RETURN TO EDEN

When her twin brother Laurie is terribly injured in a tractor accident, Amber Wakefield has to return to face the memories of her past. She cannot forget discovering that her fiancé, Rory Ashton, was having an affair with Laurie's wife, and now blames them both for the accident that has left her brother in a coma. Laurie had become careless of his own safety after the revelation of his wife's affair, and although Rory assures Amber that he no longer loves Zoe, but her, she doesn't know if she can ever trust him again. As her brother fights for his life, Amber struggles with her feelings. Should she believe Rory once more, or should she give her love to Fergus Carew, the local vet who has been a tower of strength to her?

RETURN TO EDEN

Margaret Allan

CHIVERS LARGE PRINT
BATH

British Library Cataloguing in Publication Data available

This Large Print edition published by Chivers Press, Bath, 1995.

Published by arrangement with Robert Hale Limited.

U.K. Hardcover   ISBN 0 7451 2571 9
U.K. Softcover   ISBN 0 7451 2575 1

Photoset, printed and bound in Great Britain by
Redwood Books, Trowbridge, Wiltshire

RETURN TO EDEN

CHAPTER ONE

The warm air in the spacious kitchen of the hotel was filled with the aroma of the spices that Amber had added to the huge bowl of cake mixture that now only needed a final stir. With the hotel empty now of tourists it had seemed a good time to bake the Christmas cakes that would be needed in a few weeks. Amber looked down at the rich mixture and sighed with satisfaction. There was only the long, slow baking to be done and she could go for a walk while that was taking place.

'They smell gorgeous, and they taste delicious,' her employer said as she scooped out a teaspoon of the mixture and ate it with enjoyment. 'There won't be much happening here until we get the pre-Christmas parties and dinners to cater for, so why don't you take that break I suggested, Amber? It will give you the chance to go and see your family, if you wish.'

'I'll think about it, Mrs Guthrie,' Amber said quietly.

The trouble was, Amber admitted to herself after Mrs Guthrie had left the kitchen, that she was afraid to visit her family. Yet one part of her longed to see Laurie and Tom because it seemed to be a lifetime since she had last seen them. Maybe that was why she could not rid herself of the worry which had been niggling

1

away inside her for so long, the gut feeling that all was not well at Edengate Farm. That there was something wrong with either Tom or Laurie. Something that would explain the uneasiness she felt when she spoke to one of them on the phone. There was nothing to stop her from going home to Edengate now, no longer the excuse that she was unable to get away from her job as cook at this luxurious small country hotel for long enough to make the journey home. Nothing except the knowledge that Rory would still be there, living so close to the farm, riding past it on Kelly, walking past it with Major. How could she go back when there was always the chance of meeting Rory face to face? How could she go back to stay in the same house as Zoe, to pretend that all was well and that Zoe had not betrayed both her and Laurie?

She felt the familiar ache deep inside her when she thought of Rory and Zoe. If it had not been for Zoe she would not have been here now in this Highland hotel struggling to make a new life for herself that was so different from the one she had planned to share with Rory. There was no sense in dwelling on what might have been though, she told herself sternly. At least she was happy for most of the time working for Mrs Guthrie, enjoying menu planning with her and trying out new dishes which tested the skills she had acquired in her years at the catering college. It was in her off-

2

duty time that she missed the people and places of the Eden Valley.

Pushing aside her homesickness with a conscious effort, she set about the task of filling the tins she had prepared earlier with the rich cake mixture, then put them into the oven to cook for four hours at a very low temperature. While they cooked she would take that walk, see if the fresh air and the exercise helped her to decide whether she was brave enough to go back to Edenby for a few days.

The trees that grew close to the shore of the small loch less than a mile from the hotel glowed a deep gold in their late autumn foliage as she strode briskly beneath them with discarded acorns crunching beneath her feet. Three hundred miles away the great oaks that grew close to the river near the Edengate Hotel would be casting colourful reflections on the water, the fells would be dressed with the burning bronze of dying bracken, they would be building the bonfire on the edge of the village ready for November 5th.

A great longing filled her to be there in the place where she had spent most of her life. She fought the longing by thinking about the package holiday she could take to laze in the sun, or the visit she could make to a friend made at catering college who had a job and a flat near London. When she headed back towards the hotel she was still trying to decide between the two and closing her mind firmly to

3

Edenby and her brothers.

Perhaps she would choose London and the company of Judith, who was such fun to be with, because the package holiday would not be much fun on her own. She quickened her footsteps as she turned into the hotel drive, looking about her for the figure of her employer, who had said she was going to plant more daffodil bulbs in the garden while the weather was mild. There was Mrs Guthrie now, coming down the front steps with a pair of gardening gloves which she lifted to wave to Amber. She smiled and waved back.

'Amber, I'm glad you are back. I was just coming to look for you,' Mrs Guthrie said breathlessly.

'Why? Is there something wrong, Mrs Guthrie?' Even as she asked the question Amber knew that there was. The face of the older woman was unsmiling, the expression in her grey eyes troubled.

'There was a telephone call from your brother a few minutes ago. He wants you to ring him back as soon as possible. I'm afraid there's been an accident my dear.'

'Oh no! Not Tom!'

Already Amber was stumbling up the steps and into the hall, heading for the telephone which stood on the handsome mahogany desk in the reception area. Her fingers shook as she tapped out the code and then the number of Edengate Farm, her throat went dry as she listened to the ringing that would be amplified so that it could be heard by anyone working in the farm buildings. The moment the ringing ceased she spoke urgently.

'Laurie! What's wrong? What's happened to Tom?'

With a deepening sense of shock she became aware that the answering voice was not that of her twin brother, Laurie, but the gruff young voice of fourteen year old Tom.

'Amber, please come home. You must come! We need you.'

Tom was struggling not to cry. Her alarm grew too strong to be contained.

'What is it, Tom? Tell me what's happened!'

'It's Laurie. He's hurt, badly hurt. He's unconscious.'

'How? How did he get hurt?'

She held her breath, willing herself to keep calm so that she could help her young brother.

'The tractor turned over, up on Top Moor. Laurie was flung out. He was—' The boy could say no more for the sobs that shook him.

Amber's legs were trembling. She held on to the desk for support as she spoke again. 'Hang on, Tom. I'll be with you just as soon as I can. I'll leave at once, but it'll take me a few hours to get home.' She paused, then added, 'Is Zoe with you?'

He sniffed loudly, trying to regain control of himself. 'No, I'm on my own.'

'I suppose Zoe's at the hospital. With

5

Laurie, I mean?'

'No, she's not. She's—' Once again he was unable to continue for the sobs that shook him.

A terrible fear took possession of Amber then. Was it already too late? Was that what Tom was trying to say to her?

'What are you saying, Tom? Is Laurie—' She could not put it into words.

'I've told you—he's critical. Please come!'

'I will, Tom. I'll leave right away, I promise.'

With that Amber put down the phone and turned to Mrs Guthrie, who was waiting close at hand to hear what it was all about.

'It's my twin, Laurie, who's been hurt, Mrs Guthrie. I'll have to go home at once because it sounds quite bad.'

'What happened? Was it a car accident?'

'No, Tom says the tractor turned over up on Top Moor, and that Laurie is unconscious.' Her face crumpled as she gave the bad news.

Mrs Guthrie put an arm about her. 'Of course you must go at once. You run upstairs and pack your bag while I make you a cup of tea.'

Barely ten minutes later, Amber was back in the kitchen carrying a suitcase and her shoulder bag. She gulped down the hot tea which the older woman had made, and tried to answer her few questions.

'Your brother is married, isn't he?'

'Yes, but Tom said Zoe wasn't there. That he needed me.' There had been something

6

worrying about the way Tom had said that. Tom liked Zoe, he didn't know she had been cheating on Laurie.

'I've filled a flask of coffee for you and made a few sandwiches for when you stop for a break. You'll need to take a break or you'll run the risk of falling asleep,' Mrs Guthrie told her.

'Yes, but I must get there quickly because Tom sounded hysterical. I got the feeling he was alone at the farm, but I can't think why Zoe left him there instead of taking him with her to the hospital. She must know how he is feeling, because he adores Laurie.'

'You'll be there in a few hours, but do drive carefully, won't you my dear?'

Amber gripped her hand gratefully as she took the carrier bag containing the flask of coffee and the packet of sandwiches. Then she remembered the cakes. 'You'll take the cakes out in a couple of hours, won't you?' Mrs Guthrie nodded. 'Yes, of course.'

'I'd like to know that you've arrived safely, if you can spare the time to give me a ring tonight. God be with you, my dear.'

With that, the kindly Scotswoman gave her a farewell wave as Amber put her car into gear and drove as fast as she dared down the long gravel drive towards the entrance gates and the road that would lead her in a few miles to the motorway, and Laurie.

It was dark by the time those long, monotonous, motorway miles were behind her

7

and she was aching, with the effort of concentrating all her attention on her driving and forcing her anxiety about Laurie to the back of her mind. Only once on the journey from Scotland did she stop, at one of the motorway service areas where she poured out coffee from the flask Mrs Guthrie had provided then dashed to the toilet while it was cooling. Inside the building she saw the public telephones and decided to ring Tom, to give him the assurance that she was on her way home.

Tom was so long in answering her call that her uneasiness threatened to get out of hand, until his breathless shout of 'Edengate Farm' hit her ears.

'It's me, Tom. I thought I'd let you know I'm near the border now so I'll be with you in a couple of hours. Is there any more news?'

'No better news. He's still in a coma, and still critical. I rang the hospital a few minutes ago before I went out to check that the animals were all right.'

'Didn't Zoe think to ring you from the hospital and let you know what was happening? I suppose she's still there with Laurie?'

'No, she isn't!' Tom's voice sounded full of anger.

'Where is she then, if she's not with you either?'

'How would I know? I told you, she's gone.'

8

Amber drew in her breath sharply. 'What do you mean, Tom?'

'You'll find out, when you get here.'

To her dismay he then slammed down the phone. Hurrying back to her car to drink the lukewarm coffee, she found herself filled with foreboding. She had been right to think there was something wrong at Edengate Farm, something wrong with Laurie, even before the news of his accident reached her. Well, in a couple of hours she'd be there to find out what it was all about, she told herself as she switched on the car engine and joined the speeding vehicles for the last stage of her journey to Edenby.

It was raining heavily when she reached the tree-lined village High Street that she knew so well and began the ascent of the hill that went steeply up and up in a series of bends, leaving the Edengate Hotel at the bottom, past scattered cottages and farm buildings until close to the top the lights of Edengate Farm appeared.

She was too weary, and too worried, to waste time opening the big farm gates so that she could drive straight into the yard. Instead she brought her car to a halt in the parking place beneath the tall pines on the edge of the forest opposite the farm, left the door unlocked and raced through the downpour to the side gate which gave foot access to the farmhouse. By then the sound of her arrival had alerted the two collies, who set up a great commotion from one of the farm buildings. A moment later the back door was flung open and she saw her younger brother waiting for her.

'Hello, Tom,' she whispered as her gaze took in the sag of his slim young shoulders and the despair written on this thin features.

'Oh, Ambie, I'm glad you're here!' His mouth trembled as he took a step towards her. Then they were hugging each other silently, too full of emotion to speak. After that the dogs burst in with a welcome for Amber of pleased barks and wildly waving plumed tails.

'Hello, Chance! Hello, Risky!' As she bent her head over the two dogs and let them lick her hands she felt a small twinge of joy run through her because at last she was back in this beloved place. Then the reason she was back pushed away all else and she asked the question that had to be asked.

'Is there any more news yet? Since I rang you from the motorway, I mean.'

'No. When you rang I thought at first it was the hospital and I was frightened,' Tom admitted. 'They said they would ring if he got any worse, when they told me it was best if I came home to wait.'

'I still don't understand about Zoe. Why you had to be on your own to go through this. Why she wasn't with you.'

'I thought I told you, on the phone, that she'd gone,' Tom said fiercely.

'Gone where?' She frowned as she waited for him to explain.

'I don't know. She just walked out and left.'

Amber drew in her breath sharply. 'You mean, left Laurie?'

'Yes.'

'When did she go?'

'I can't remember the exact date. A few weeks ago.'

'Yet you never said anything to me. Either of you.' Her voice was accusing.

Tom shifted his feet uncomfortably on the red tiled kitchen floor and avoided her eyes as he told her the reason for his silence.

'Laurie didn't want you to know. He said I was not to tell you if I spoke to you on the phone.'

'Didn't she leave an address? Somewhere she could be contacted?' Amber persisted. Had Zoe gone away alone, the thought came to her then, or had she gone with Rory? She wanted to ask Tom, but she could not get the words out yet.

Tom pushed a lock of thick fair hair back from his forehead and continued to stare down at the puddle of muddy water that had collected around his feet. 'I don't know. Laurie didn't seem to want to talk about it. He just told me, when I came in from school one day, that she had said she was not going to spend another winter here, packed her cases and gone.'

11

Amber took off her damp jacket and hung it close to the solid fuel range to dry. She needed time to frame her next question. Time to prepare herself for the answer she might get.

'Did she—was she—going away on her own, Tom?' she asked at last.

The question hung between them while Tom shuffled his feet again, then grabbed a towel from the airer and began to mop the water from his hair. He knew what she was getting at, and was uncomfortable with that knowledge.

'Like I said, I wasn't here when she went.'

'You must have been surprised. Shocked maybe? Both you and Laurie,' she suggested tentatively.

'I think Laurie was shocked, but I wasn't surprised when I found she had gone,' he told her as he flung the towel onto the back of a chair.

'Why weren't you surprised, Tom?' she asked quietly. She felt certain he had had no idea that Zoe had been meeting Rory in secret, and she was sure that Laurie had not known either because Zoe had asked her to say nothing. Because she did not want to see Laurie hurt she had agreed to keep quiet.

'I was not surprised at her leaving because I knew they'd been arguing more and more often after you went to work in Scotland. They always seemed to be having rows, but usually in the end Laurie gave in and did what she wanted. I supposed they must have had a worse

12

row than ever that day about Zoe wanting to go to Spain for a holiday and Laurie saying they couldn't leave the farm. I think he expected her to come back at first, when she had been away for a few days. Then he stopped talking about it and I knew she wouldn't come back.'

'I don't understand why he didn't tell me about it when we talked on the phone.' Of course she had never asked about Zoe; she could not bring herself to do that.

'He didn't want you to know,' Tom said again. 'He said I was not to tell you.'

'Why? I had to know sometime—'

'He was afraid you might think you had to come rushing back here to look after us,' Tom admitted then. 'He said that would not be fair to you now that you'd made a new life for yourself in Scotland and found a job you liked.'

'I guessed there was something wrong. I've been worried about you both for weeks.'

As she finished speaking Amber's gaze moved about the farmhouse kitchen and found ample evidence that there had been no woman in the house for some time. Neglect was everywhere to be seen; in dishes left to soak since goodness knew when, in grease encrusted worktops and grimy kitchen towels, while the red tiled floor was covered with mud and straw.

'I said we ought to ask you to come home, but Laurie wouldn't listen. He said we must

13

manage as best we could. That it was best if you didn't know.'

'Was he terribly upset? I suppose he would be—'

'What do you think? You know how he always was about her, ever since he first brought her here. He didn't talk about it though, he just never mentioned her name. He told me, just once, that he was not going to talk about it to anyone. But he was always thinking about her because if I asked him anything he quite often didn't even seem to have heard me.'

'Poor Laurie! I expect he was devastated.'

'He was really shut inside himself, and he had got very careless about things lately. The sort of things he had always told me to be specially careful about. Like going up on Top Moor with the tractor.'

Tom's voice began to shake. Amber knew he was close to breaking down as he went on. 'Laurie told me never to risk using a tractor up on Top Moor because the rocks made it so dangerous, but that's what he was doing this morning when the accident happened; using a tractor on Top Moor where the biggest rocks are! That was stupid of him, wasn't it? Really stupid!'

Distress was building up in the boy again. Amber put her arms about him and tried to comfort him with soothing words even though she too thought Laurie had been foolish to use a tractor in a place where their father had

14

always said it was unsafe to do so.

'It was an accident, Tom, and accidents do happen on farms. You know they do.'

'This one shouldn't have happened. I told you, he's been getting careless because he doesn't care what happens now that she's not here. I hate her!'

Not half as much as I hate her, Amber added silently as she moved away from her brother and went to fill the electric kettle at the sink. 'I'll make us some tea, Tom, then we'll both feel better,' she told him. 'And I'll ring the hospital while I'm waiting for the kettle to boil. There might be some better news by now.'

There was no better news. Just the information that Laurie was still deeply unconscious, and still critically ill.

'I've driven down from Scotland to see him, can I come at once?' she asked.

The voice on the other end of the line softened. 'I know you'll be anxious, but best to wait until morning if you've already had a long drive. There'll be no change before then. We could do with the address of his wife though, if you could let us have it. She ought to be informed about what's happened.'

'I'll see if I can find out where she is.' With a sigh, Amber put down the phone.

'There's no fresh news, Tom,' she said as she made the tea, 'but they want Zoe's address at the hospital so we must try and find out where she went.'

15

'You'd better ring the hotel.' He did not look at her as he said that. 'I expect the Ashtons know where she is.'

Amber clenched her hands. She did not want to have to ring the Edengate Hotel and speak to Rory, but what else could she do? If she was lucky it would be Henry, Rory's father, who answered. She drew a long breath of relief when she heard his voice saying the name of the hotel.

'Henry, it's Amber Wakefield,' she began hesitantly.

'Amber, my dear! This is a surprise, I didn't know you were home.'

'I've only just arrived. I came as soon as I heard about the accident.'

Henry would be standing in the beautiful oak-panelled hall of the Edengate Hotel. There would be a great bowl of chrysanthemums standing on the reception desk and a log fire blazing in the hearth. If it had not been for Zoe she would have been living at the hotel now, helping Rory and his father to run it. She would have been Rory's wife...

'The accident? I'm not with you, my dear. I only got home an hour or so ago from a meeting in Durham so I'm not up to date with the news. Is it young Tom?'

'No, it's Laurie. The tractor turned over this morning and he was flung out and terribly injured. He's in a coma and his condition is critical Henry.'

16

She heard his shocked gasp, then his words of sympathy. 'How terrible for you. Is there any way I can help? You only have to say...'

Amber swallowed. 'I don't think there's anything any of us can do at the moment, Henry, but I rang you because I wondered if you had any idea where Zoe was. The hospital wants her address.'

There was silence for a moment while she tensed her body and waited for his answer. Or for him to hand her over to Rory.

'I'm afraid I can't help you, Amber, and Rory isn't here at the moment. He's taking some time off while things are quiet. I wish I could help you, my dear.'

His voice was full of the compassion he felt for her. Amber knew he felt badly about what had happened between her and Rory. He was a kindly man and she had always liked him.

'If you think it might help, I'll let Rory know about the accident and see if he can help.'

Suddenly her affection for Henry Ashton was replaced by an unexpected burst of fury brought on by her extreme tiredness and anxiety.

'We don't need to pretend with each other, do we Henry?' she said hotly. 'You know as well as I do that Zoe walked out on Laurie because of Rory, so he'll know where she is. I want her to come back, Henry, so that she is here when Laurie comes out of his coma. She owes him that much. Will you give her that

17

message for me?'

She did not wait for his answer. Instead she slammed down the phone so that she could mop up the tears that were streaming down her face.

CHAPTER TWO

Before going back into the farmhouse kitchen to Tom, Amber stumbled wearily up the stairs to wash her face so that he would not be distressed by her tears. She felt better after doing that and able to respond quite cheerfully to Tom's shout that he had poured the tea. Downstairs again, she faced him calmly.

'It was Henry who answered the phone,' she told him. 'He said Rory was away.'

Tom scowled. 'I thought he might be. I can guess where.'

Amber let that pass. 'Henry is going to get in touch with him and ask him to pass a message on to Zoe that she must come back at once.'

His scowl deepened. 'Do we have to have her back?' he muttered.

Amber sighed. 'Yes, Tom. Because when Laurie comes out of his coma he might ask for her.'

'If he has any sense he won't want anything more to do with her.'

'It's not a matter of having sense, Tom,' she

18

tried to explain. 'It's—something quite different.' How could you expect a fourteen years old to understand that you could still love a person even if you no longer liked and trusted them? 'We don't know how he'll be when he comes out of it. We have to do what is best for him, even if it's very hard for us,' she went on.

It was more than hard for her to even contemplate living in the same house as Zoe. How she would face up to it she dare not think, since their last meeting had been a very stormy one in which she had accused her sister-in-law of wrecking both her own life and Laurie's.

Zoe had laughed at that and told her not to be so melodramatic. 'I'm still here with Laurie even if I am bored out of my mind, and he's quite happy because he has no idea I've been meeting Rory. As for Rory and you, that never would have worked because you are not really his type at all. So I've saved you from making a ghastly mistake,' she had replied with a coolness which had infuriated Amber.

Amber had blown her top then and told her exactly what she thought about her, ending with the statement that she wouldn't ever return to Edengate Farm while her sister-in-law was there.

Zoe had shrugged that off lightly and said 'That's up to you, isn't it?'

Tom knew nothing about that confrontation, he had been at school when it had taken place and Laurie had been away at a farm auction. Neither of her brothers knew, either, about what had caused the ill feeling between herself and Zoe and driven her away from Edenby and to the job in Scotland.

They did not know of the day she had made the discovery that Zoe was deceiving Laurie. The day she had accidentally run into a puppy while on a shopping trip to Barndale and carried it into a country inn on the moorland road to await the arrival of the vet. She had been crouching over the little creature trying to comfort it when the sound of Zoe's laughter had drifted out to her from an adjoining room. When she opened the door into that room she had seen Zoe, who was supposed to be visiting an elderly aunt in a nursing home in Barndale, sitting with a young and handsome man. They were so totally immersed in one another that they were oblivious of her presence. She had wanted to turn her back on them and run away; to pretend it was not Rory sitting there hanging on to Zoe's every word, showing so plainly by his body language that he desired her. Yet she remained rooted to the spot with her throat swelling until the puppy had given a loud yelp of pain and leapt across the room, bringing Rory to his feet, startled and with a face full of guilt.

She could not remember just what he had said as they confronted one another across the parlour of the inn for a long moment, but she knew Zoe had said nothing. Then the arrival of the vet had put an end to the impossible situation and she had found herself being led out into the back of the premises along with the puppy by the young, brown haired, sturdy man whose presence helped her to gain control of herself again. They had gone out into the garden of the inn and the vet had gently examined the injured dog while she stood by wishing with all her heart that she had not chosen to travel to Barndale on that particular day.

'He's been lucky,' the young man in the baggy Aran sweater told her when the examination was over. 'There doesn't seem to be much damage done, except for his gashed thigh, but I'll take him into my surgery and give him an X ray to make sure, if that's all right with you?'

She was startled, 'He's not my dog. He ran out in front of my car and I couldn't avoid hitting him. I don't know who he belongs to. He hasn't got an address on his collar.'

The vet's face sobered. 'Poor little devil, that means he could have been dumped from a car by someone who wanted to get rid of him.'

Amber shuddered. 'They nearly did! I thought I had killed him at first. Until he got to his feet and began to wander about. How could they do that to him?'

The brown haired man shrugged his heavy shoulders. 'It happens all too often, I'm afraid.

21

Of course it could just be that he's escaped from his home and got lost. I'll get in touch with the police and see if he's been reported missing.'

For a moment the plight of the dog claimed all her sympathy and left her no time for thinking about herself. 'I'll pay the bill for his treatment if you'll send it to me. Amber Wakefield, Edengate Farm, Edenby.'

'Oh, I was out there a couple of weeks ago but I don't remember seeing you there.' His voice was warm and friendly.

'I expect I was at work.'

'Better luck next time, I hope.'

That was said with a grin, but Amber did not respond. Instead she stumbled away from him towards one of the picnic tables that were set in the garden because she was losing her control again and did not want to embarrass him. There she remained, biting on her bottom lip and clenching her hands as she struggled to pull herself together. She had no idea that the vet was still there until he pushed a steaming cup of coffee across to her and seated himself opposite her.

'You'll feel better when you've drunk this,' he said gently. 'Please don't upset yourself, I'm sure it wasn't your fault.'

She gulped and reached for the coffee with shaking hands, spilling a little before she managed to drink any.

'You really must not blame yourself,' he

tried to comfort her. 'Dogs running loose are always a hazard, and it isn't as if he has been badly hurt. He'll be fine again in a couple of days.'

He thought she was crying over the plight of the dog, she realized then. He was not to know that it was the picture of Rory sitting too close to Zoe in the room behind them that was filling her with grief. Nor could she tell him about that. All she could do was gulp down the rest of the coffee he had so thoughtfully provided for her, then tell him unsteadily that she felt much better now and must be on her way. She ended by telling him how grateful she was for his help, and even managed a wavering smile as she added. 'Don't forget to send me your bill, will you Mr—?'

'Carew. Fergus Carew,' he introduced himself. 'I joined the practice just before Mr Middleton retired. As I said, don't worry about the puppy too much. Are you sure you are feeling well enough to drive?'

'Yes, thank you. I must go or I'll never manage to get all my shopping done. I have a buffet party to prepare for this evening at the Country Club where I work. Goodbye, Mr Carew.'

'Goodbye for now,' he answered, as though he expected to meet her again before long.

As Amber walked through the inn to where she had left her car she had to pass the room where she had seen Rory with Zoe. A swift

23

glance through the open door showed her that they had gone, so she would not have to face them again just yet, she thought with a surge of relief. Later, when she had decided what she was going to say to Rory, would be soon enough.

As she resumed her interrupted journey and headed for Barndale she tried to push the thought of that meeting out of her mind. They would both try to provide her with a rational explanation of why they were there together when Zoe was supposed to be visiting the very sick aunt whom she had told them often did not even know what day of the week it was, but their attitude towards one another in those moments when she had watched them unobserved had told her all she needed to know.

What if Laurie should find out that they were meeting, the thought came to her then because she was certain this was not their first such meeting? Small incidents were coming into her mind, times she had dropped into the farm unexpectedly and found Rory there, but not Laurie because Laurie was away at some cattle auction or farm sale. Times when she had been off duty from her job at the Country Club but Rory had made vague excuses about why he could not join her. The way he had stopped talking about the wedding they had begun to plan for next spring...

Laurie would be devastated if he discovered

24

that Zoe was cheating on him. That thought haunted Amber all the way to Barndale, and again as she drove back. Before meeting Zoe, Laurie had lived for the farm and his hobby of sheepdog trialling. Once he had met her he was besotted by her and would not rest until he had persuaded her to marry him. Amber thought he had been in too much of a hurry to get married, and was amazed that Zoe, who was devoted to her career as a model and promotions girl, had allowed herself to be talked into it. Zoe was not domesticated and was absent from the farm from time to time to fulfil her career commitments and at those times Amber would cook for her brothers as she had done before Laurie's marriage.

What should she do, she asked herself as she neared Edengate Farm at the end of her shopping trip? Before she did anything she must talk to Zoe, see what she had to say, even though she dreaded the encounter. She pulled into the farm entrance, hoping that Laurie would be away checking the sheep on the fells now that lambing time was close.

As she had hoped, Laurie was out with his dogs and the Land Rover, but Zoe was waiting for her, ready with her explanation.

'Sorry we couldn't wait and have a drink with you this afternoon, Amber. I just ran into Rory there when I was on my way to see Aunt Lydia.'

Amber was just as ready with her angry

25

response. 'It didn't take you long to get close to him, did it?'

'What do you mean, Amber?' Zoe raised brilliant green eyes in a look that should have been innocent, but was not.

'You know perfectly well what I mean. I'd been watching you for some time before you even saw me, and if you expect me to believe that was your first such meeting you must think I'm very naive. Rory was all over you, and you were enjoying it. I wonder now just how many times you've been together, and why I never suspected you before when I've found Rory here while Laurie has been out.'

Zoe shrugged her slim shoulders elegantly. 'So it's no good me denying we've been enjoying one another's company, is it? You aren't going to say anything to Laurie though, are you? Because Laurie wouldn't understand. Laurie doesn't realize how bored I get with country life, and he's always busy with the farm.'

'What makes you think I understand?' Amber hit back.

'Well,' Zoe said slowly, 'you know Rory, don't you?'

'What's that supposed to mean?'

'I mean you know how attractive he is. How hard he is to resist.'

Amber's throat went dry. 'Go on.'

'Rory knew how bored I was getting with too much of the country life, so he suggested we meet up for a drink when I was going to see Aunt Lydia.'

'But neither of you thought to mention it, did you?' Rory had not mentioned it when Amber had proposed that they go into Barndale together today, have some lunch and look at furniture. That really hurt. 'It wasn't the first time you had met away from here, was it?' she challenged Zoe.

Before Zoe could either confirm or deny her statement there came the sound of the Land Rover entering the yard accompanied by the barking of the two sheepdogs. Zoe's face filled with relief that the confrontation had been interrupted, then she turned abruptly away from Amber and walked quickly into the farmhouse.

Amber remained where she was, closing her lips on her bitterness and disgust as her brother jumped down from the driving seat and came towards her.

'Hi, Amber!' he greeted her. 'It looks like being a good lambing season this year. Nice mild weather and the ewes looking healthy. I'm starving, I hope Zoe's got something good for tea. Are you coming in for some?'

Laurie looked so happy, so full of pleasure with the way things were going in his life, how could she bear to wipe the joy from his eyes? How could she stay for tea and share the meal with Zoe, pretending that all was well between them?

27

'No, I can't Laurie. There's a buffet party for the Rotary Club tonight so I'm working. I'll be seeing you soon.'

With that she hurried to her car and drove away from the farm as fast as she dared before she could change her mind and tell her brother that his wife was cheating on him. Let Zoe stew in her own anxiety about whether she would tell Laurie what she had seen, she thought bitterly. Why shouldn't she suffer too?

She was not surprised when Rory rang her soon after her arrival back at the Country Club while she was working on the buffet food. He came straight to the point, for which she was thankful.

'What time will you be free, Amber? I think we need to have a talk, don't you?' he said without preamble.

'Yes. You have some questions to answer, Rory, don't you?'

'I can explain, if you'll just give me a chance. So what time shall I pick you up?' he persisted.

'Not before nine.' She could not bear to say anything else to him. In fact could hardly bear to talk to him at all for the anger that consumed her.

'I'll see you then, darling.'

How could he, she raged after she had slammed the phone down, speak to her in that soft caressing tone when only a few hours ago she had found him with Zoe, his whole attitude showing how he felt about her sister-in-law.

28

Maybe they were already lovers? This last thought filled her with revulsion.

Dazed with unhappiness, she made herself go on with the task of finishing the lavish buffet food while the hands of the clock began to crawl towards nine o'clock. At last everything was done, the table looked superb with a sumptuous selection of trifles, cheesecakes, and pavlovas set out to follow the cold meats and various salads and pickles. There was nothing more she could do, except go to her room and get ready for her meeting with Rory.

When she was ready she took a long, appraising look at herself in the mirror of her dressing table. Her smoky blue linen suit was almost new and fitted her well, her brown hair shone about her clear-skinned face, but apart from her deep blue eyes she knew that her features were unremarkable. That she could not compete with the stunning attractiveness of Zoe. Yet Rory had chosen her, before Laurie brought Zoe to Edengate Farm.

Rory was waiting for her in the lounge bar of the club, talking to an acquaintance as he sipped a beer. She watched him from the doorway for a moment, her heart aching with loss at the sight of his handsome profile, his tall and slender body that was so graceful in every movement that he made. It would be hard for her to give him up, but she knew she was about to do that.

As the thought crossed her mind, Rory

turned his head and saw her coming towards him. Immediately then he put down his drink, made his excuses to the man he had been talking to, and came to usher her out of the club to the car park where his car waited.

'We can have a drink somewhere else,' he told her.

This suited her well enough, because she had no wish to have things out with Rory in a place where they were both so well known. She remained silent as he opened the passenger door for her and slid into the driving seat beside her before sending the low-slung sports model speeding along the moorland road at a pace that made her hold her breath since she knew that some of the sheep that grazed on Middleby Moor were inclined to wander into the road. She was relieved when he reduced his speed at last and steered the vehicle into a parking bay in one of the picnic areas which gave such wonderful views of the fell scenery in daylight. Now the daylight had gone and the atmosphere was misty and murky with a fine rain falling.

When the noise of the engine had died away he sat for a moment with his hands resting on the steering wheel, frowning as he attempted to marshall his thoughts into the right sort of words.

'I suppose you were surprised at seeing me with Zoe this afternoon,' he began at last. 'Did she tell you that I ran into her there when I stopped for a drink on my way to pick up some stuff for the hotel from Barndale?'

Amber gave an exclamation of disgust. 'I wonder just how many times you've run into one another like that when she was supposed to be visiting her old auntie who is so confused she doesn't know whether Zoe is there or not.'

'What do you mean?' he said uneasily.

'I mean that Zoe's explanation was that you thought it might help her to cope with her boredom with farm life if you met her for a drink.'

A frown darkened his features again. 'I knew you wouldn't understand if I mentioned it to you, so I didn't bother. She really does get lonely, poor kid, living in that isolated farm with Laurie working all hours, Tom away at school and you at the Country Club, so you can't blame her for needing a bit of company.'

'She isn't a poor kid!' Amber snapped. 'She's a married woman and she gets away from the farm sometimes if she can get promotion work locally. She's Laurie's wife, and I don't want to see him get hurt.'

'Then he should take her out more often, then she wouldn't get so bored.'

'How can he, when this is one of the busiest times of the year for him? In any case, I wouldn't have thought Zoe's state of mind was anything to do with you, Rory. I would have thought, or assumed, that it was my state of mind you were most concerned with. My

31

happiness, if you like.'

'I am concerned about you. You know I am.'

She shook her head slowly, sadly. 'No, you are not, Rory. Not like you used to be before Zoe came here.'

There was a certain relief in bringing into the open something she had been worrying over in recent weeks, the puzzlement she had been feeling because some of the sparkle had gone from the way Rory spoke to her or touched her. Of course, their's had been a long engagement. Perhaps too long...

'You've been different ever since Laurie brought Zoe to the farm for good. You've been looking for excuses to visit there when I wasn't there. Especially when I wasn't there, I think, as well as when Laurie was away too. I think you've lost interest in our wedding plans too since Zoe came. Or maybe you've just lost interest in me?'

The lump which had been forming in her throat as she uttered the words threatened to choke her as she waited for him to reply. To deny her last two statements. How could he do that though when the truth was written all over his handsome features?

'Maybe we've waited too long to get married? Perhaps we should have done it earlier.'

'When I was at college, you mean? Neither of us thought that was the right thing to do, did we? Then when I finished at college Mum was ill and we knew she would never be well enough to cope with the farmhouse again so Laurie needed me to help him.'

'I needed you too, but you put your brother first.'

'Both Tom and Laurie needed me, and I had promised Mum I'd look after them until Laurie got married. I had no choice, Rory, and we started planning our wedding as soon as Laurie married Zoe.'

He sighed. 'I don't think there's any point in going over all that old ground. We are talking about now, what's going to happen now. You don't believe I was just having a drink with her, do you? You think it's more than that.'

'I know it's more than that. It's ages since you sat so close to me when we had a drink together, and a long time since you looked at me the way you were looking at her. I'm not blind, Rory, and I'm not that naive either. You fancy her, and she fancies you. How much further than that it's gone I don't know—'

She waited for him to deny that it had gone any further than those scorching looks she had seen exchanged between him and Zoe at the inn but the words never came so she was forced to draw her own conclusions.

'What are you going to do, tell Laurie?' he said in a low voice when the silence had become unbearable.

She shook her head. 'No, I couldn't bear to do that to him. He thinks she's so perfect. What

33

do you and Zoe intend to do about it?'

He looked surprised at the question. 'Nothing. She was bored, and I was tempted. That's all there was to it. I suppose it has to end now that you know.'

'If it doesn't end I will tell Laurie,' she said, and meant it.

'I don't know what to say, how to tell you how sorry I am—'

'Don't bother to begin, just drive me back to the Country Club, please.'

It was an uncomfortable journey during which she willed herself to stay in control, not to give way to her feelings in front of him. In fact she appeared quite calm when, as they stopped in the car park of the club, she slipped off the ring he had given her for their engagement and placed it on the dashboard. Then without looking at him or uttering another word she left him.

By the next morning she knew that she must get away from Edenby as soon as possible. By the end of the month she had a new job in Scotland and a new way of life without either Rory or her brothers. She had even found some contentment in that way of life, until the terrible news of Laurie's accident reached her.

Now she was back in Edenby, and she must try to make Zoe come back so that Laurie would have something to live for. If he managed to go on living.

CHAPTER THREE

When Amber arrived at the hospital the next morning to see Laurie she first had an interview with the doctor who was in charge of his case. After telling her that as yet there was no change in her brother's condition, the doctor went on to say that they could not be certain about the extent of his injuries until he had been examined by a neuro-surgeon.

'A neuro-surgeon,' Amber whispered, with her mind full of dread. 'Does that mean you think he has brain damage?'

The doctor watched her with compassionate eyes. 'He may have, we can't be certain yet. We'll be able to tell you more after Mr Richards has seen him, later today.' He paused, then went on, 'I believe your brother is married?'

She nodded, guessing what was coming next. 'I'm trying to get in touch with his wife. She's—she's on holiday abroad.'

'I expect she'll come back as soon as she is able,' he said gently.

'Yes.' Would Zoe come rushing back when she heard about the accident to Laurie? There was a doubt in her mind about that, but she could not share it with the doctor. 'Thank you for looking after him, doctor,' she said instead.

'Sister Campbell will take you to see him

now,' the doctor said, turning to smile at Tom who stood beside her, silent and white-faced.

As they followed the young nursing sister into the section of the Intensive Care Unit where Laurie was being cared for Amber found herself reaching out for Tom's hand and holding it tightly as they approached the still figure of her twin brother who lay in the high, narrow hospital bed surrounded by monitoring devices.

'Only a few minutes, I'm afraid, this morning. Mr Richards will be here to see him soon.'

Then the sister left them to stare down at Laurie in anguish because it seemed to them both that anyone who looked as ill as he did could not possibly survive. They hung on to one another's hands, neither able to speak. Their mouths were dry, their throats too swollen for words as they listened to the unfamiliar sounds that filled the warm air about them. Sounds that reminded them too vividly of the last days of their mother's illness.

At one time Tom swayed and seemed about to collapse. Amber moved quickly then to put her arm about him, to steady him against her own body, to share with him the strength and courage she had not known until then that she possessed.

'It'll be all right, Tom,' she whispered, then heard with relief the voice of the sister asking them to leave as the neuro-surgeon had arrived.

'Can we wait and hear what he says?' she asked as they moved away from Laurie's bed.

Sister Campbell shook her head. 'No, he won't have anything to tell you today. It will be best if you go home and try to get on with your lives as normally as possible,' she advised in her soft Scottish accent. 'Your brother is a farmer, isn't he? So there will be animals to be cared for and other things you can do to help him. It could be some time before there is any change in his condition, but you'll be able to come in and see him this evening.'

Amber thanked her, then tucked her arm into Tom's and led him out into the corridor and from there to where her car waited in the hospital car park. She could feel him trembling and did not want him to break down until they were away from everyone else.

'How can we just get on with our lives normally when Laurie looks as if he's going to die!' he burst out when they were inside the car and she was about to drive off.

Amber winced. She would not let herself dwell on the possibility that Laurie might die. He was only twenty-four. He was too young to die, wasn't he?

'Laurie isn't going to die, Tom!' she said fiercely. 'He's going to get better, even if it does take a long time, and we must keep the farm going for him ready for when he comes home again. So the sooner we get back to Edengate and start doing that, the more we'll be helping Laurie. Right?'

She gripped Tom's shoulder as she said that, and watched the crumpled, boyish face take on a look of resolution.

'Right!' he echoed huskily.

As they entered the farmhouse kitchen the phone began to ring out in the hall. Stifling the alarm that flared inside her Amber hurried to answer it. It couldn't be the hospital, could it, not when they'd only just come from there? Her breath was expelled on a great burst of relief when she heard the deep voice of Henry Ashton speaking to her from the Edengate Hotel, to ask about Laurie.

'He's about the same, Henry, still critically ill. We were able to see him for a few minutes, Tom and I. Then we had to leave because they had brought a neuro-surgeon in to examine him, to find out if he had suffered any brain damage. They told us to come home and get on with our lives as normally as possible, as it could be a long time before there is any change in his condition.'

'I'm so sorry you are having to go through all this. Is there anything I can do to help? You only have to ask, my dear.'

'There might be something, when I get round to thinking straight again, Henry, but right now I can't think of anything. Other than getting the message to Zoe that she must come back; that the doctor who is looking after

38

Laurie thinks she ought to come.'

Amber waited, knowing that by now Henry would surely have had time to get in touch with Rory, and maybe even with Zoe.

'I've been in touch with Rory, and he's promised to pass on the message to Zoe,' she was relieved to hear him say. 'I impressed on him how serious the accident was and how vital you felt it was that Zoe should return. So now it's up to her. There's nothing more I can do.'

Amber bit her lip. 'Yes, now it's up to her. I hope she'll come, for Laurie's sake.' She paused, then went on 'I didn't even know she had left, until I got home yesterday. Laurie hadn't told me, and he'd asked Tom not to say anything. I suppose he didn't want me to come rushing back, though I had a feeling there was something wrong.'

Henry Ashton sighed. 'It's been a bad business. I can't tell you how sorry I am that you should have to go through all this.'

Amber felt her throat tighten. 'Please don't say any more, Henry—'

'If only there were some way in which I could help make it up to you. You will ask, if there is anything?'

'Yes, Henry.'

Rory's father was kind and she had a deep affection for him but what could he, or anyone, do to lift the great burden of worry that seemed to be weighing her down? All she could hope for was that the message Henry had passed on

39

to Zoe would bring her speedily back to Edengate before Laurie regained consciousness. If he ever did...

To keep her most sombre thoughts at bay she set about some of the work on the farm, gathering in the eggs there had not been time to collect that morning and realizing as she did so that Tom had not eaten yet, and neither had she. She was still not hungry, but young Tom must be ravenous. It would have to be ham and eggs, she decided, with plenty of chips, because her swift glances into the pantry and the deep freezer had revealed that part of a ham was just about the only food available until she could get to the village shops.

Her nose curled with disgust as she surveyed the littered worktops and the grease-encrusted cooker. All the evidence pointed to the fact that Zoe had either been gone for some time or that she had lost all interest and pride in her home long before she had made the decision to abandon it.

Soon the large beautifully fitted kitchen which Laurie had spent so much money on to satisfy Zoe was filled with the delicious aroma of grilling ham. As soon as they had eaten she would start cleaning up, for now there was Tom to be fed, and maybe herself as well.

'That smells good. I'm starving!' he announced as he barged into the kitchen.

'How long is it since you last ate?' she asked with a smile.

40

'Breakfast yesterday, I think,' he answered with a grin.

A sudden thought came to her as she lifted an egg from the pan to transfer to his plate. 'Did you remember to feed the dogs, Tom?' she asked as one of the collies barked out in the yard.

He frowned. 'I think I fed them last night, but I'm not sure. I was in such a state that I can't really remember what I did.' He looked at her with eyes full of dismay. Always on this farm the welfare of the animals came first. It had been their father's rule, passed on to Laurie and then to Tom, and never broken.

'I'll give them something as soon as we've finished eating, in case you forgot. If you didn't, I don't suppose they'll mind fitting in an extra meal, do you?'

'No!' he grinned, then his face sobered. 'They'll be missing Laurie, won't they? I mean, he's always here with them as a rule.'

'Yes. They'll be uneasy.'

Already Tom had cleared his plate. 'That was great, Ambie. You're a better cook than Zoe. I don't think she was interested in cooking.'

'She hadn't had my training,' Amber pointed out, trying to be fair to her sister-in-law. 'You don't need to be able to cook to be a successful model or promotions girl, and I suppose she was good at her job.'

Laurie had met Zoe when she was doing

41

promotion work at the Great Yorkshire Show three years ago. Normally he would only have been there on the first day, but after meeting Zoe he had gone back on the second day, then the third to persuade her to go out with him.

'I'll feed the dogs now, while you finish your meal,' Tom's voice broke into her thoughts. Already he was on his feet and going to the pantry to find tins of meat and the bag of dogmeal. Then he carried out the two bowls to the back porch where the dogs always ate. A moment later he was back to ask, 'Have you seen Chance?'

She shook her head. 'I saw her last night when I arrived, but I don't remember seeing her this morning.'

'I'd better keep whistling for her. It's not like her not to come for her food.'

'Wasn't she fastened up with Risky when we left for the hospital?'

'I thought she was, but she seems to have slipped her collar.'

Tom marched out again as Amber began to gather up the used crockery and carry it to the sink. As she set about washing the dishes she could hear him whistling the dog, using the piercing, distinctive sound that would usually bring either of the dogs to him immediately. Only on this occasion there was no answering high-pitched bark as the dog raced homewards. She turned, frowning, to face her brother as he came back into the kitchen with a worried face.

'Where can she have got to?'

'I don't know. I'll have to find her or Laurie will think I'm not looking after things properly while he's not here. She would go missing just now, when Hendersons are due to come for the potatoes they ordered and the heifers Laurie bought on Tuesday are due for delivery.'

'I'll go and look for her, if you like,' Amber offered. 'I can catch up on the dishes later.'

Already Amber was thinking ahead as she dried her hands, wondering where she might start to look for Chance. If it had been Risky who had gone missing she would have been certain that he was visiting at some neighbouring farm where there was a bitch, but Chance never strayed far from the farm and her master. She was devoted to Laurie, who had taken her from a breeder of good dogs who had felt she had little chance of surviving. Chance had survived, thanks to Laurie's care, and proved to be a quick learner and a tireless worker with the sheep. Although small, she was tough enough to cover many miles of steep fell country when shepherding the hundreds of Swaledale sheep belonging to Edengate Farm in rain, snow, ice or wind.

A fresh worry began to niggle at Amber as she slipped on an old anorak she kept for work about the farm. Was Chance lying injured somewhere on the fells? There were many hazards there, ranging from illegal traps and

43

barbed wire fences to old mine shafts, to say nothing of the roads that dissected the area. She shivered, then felt her heart plummet as she saw a police van coming to a halt outside the farm. As she watched, a policeman left the driving seat and came towards her. It was a man who had known her family for years.

'How's Laurie?' were his first words, while his eyes showed his concern for her.

'About the same, still critical. He's being examined by a neuro-surgeon to see if he's suffered any brain damage.'

The middle-aged policeman shook his head sadly. 'It's a bad business, and no mistake.'

'Do you know exactly what happened, Jim? Can you tell me?' she pleaded.

He shook his head again. 'No, I can't lass. We don't even know exactly when the accident occurred. All we got was a report from a motorist who had noticed an overturned tractor as he drove past the parking place on Top Moor. When I got up there I found Laurie had been flung out. It looked as though he had struck his head on one of the big rocks up there. I was surprised to see him with a tractor up there, I wouldn't have thought it was the place to use one.'

'Dad always warned him about it, and Laurie wasn't usually careless,' she said thoughtfully.

'I suppose there's always the chance the dog got in his way and he turned the tractor over

44

trying to avoid it. Though it's best not to do too much speculating at this stage,' the policeman warned her.

'The dogs often went with him,' she said. Then she remembered that Chance was missing. 'You haven't seen Chance anywhere on your travels, have you Jim?'

'Not today. I saw her at the scene of the accident yesterday. She was standing guard over Laurie, then, but when the helicopter came for him it must have frightened her because she ran away as fast as she could go. Has she been missing ever since then?'

'No, she was here when I arrived last night but she had gone when we came back from the hospital this morning. I was just setting out to look for her when you came.'

'Well, I'll be on my way and I'll keep my eyes skinned for a sight of her as I go. I thought I'd just give you a call as I was passing. See if there was anything I can do to help you and young Tom. You'll let me know if there is, won't you lass?'

His kindness warmed Amber. 'Yes, of course I will, and thanks, Jim.'

As soon as the police van had driven off, Amber backed her own car out of the yard and headed up the hill towards Top Moor, travelling slowly enough to scan the countryside about her for any sign of the missing dog. She halted briefly at the gates of farms on the way, but though there were

45

sheepdogs to be seen they were not the one she was looking for so she moved on and on up the winding moorland road until she came to the parking area which gave such spectacular views of the wonderful fell scenery. An estate car was pulling into it as she drew near and as she watched a man leapt out of the driving seat and without bothering to lock the car began to scramble swiftly down the steep hillside. Inside the car a dog began to bark like mad.

Without stopping to think, Amber pulled her own car into the layby and got out to see what was happening. Then the blood drained from her face as she saw the overturned tractor, the newest and best of the tractors that belonged to Edengate Farm lying on its side in a deep rock lined gulley. Beside it, with her head resting on her paws, was Chance.

Her heart gave a great lurch of alarm when she saw Chance spring to her feet and begin to warn off the man who was striding purposefully down and down into the gulley. She held her breath as the man went on, quite unperturbed it seemed by the threatening noises being made by the sheepdog as she stood guard over her master's tractor. Then she gathered all her breath together and shouted to the dog.

'Chance! Chance! Come here lass!'

Momentarily diverted, the dog glanced upwards and recognized her, wagged her tail and looked pleased. By then the brown haired man had reached the overturned tractor and the dog turned her attention to him again and began to circle round him barking madly. She would have to get down there, Amber thought, in case Chance turned from barking to nipping.

Hastily she began the descent of the slope, calling to Chance as she did so, and slipping and sliding as she went. From time to time Chance looked up at her and wagged her tail, but she would not be diverted from her main purpose of guarding her master's property until Amber was close enough to catch her by the collar and speak sternly to her. The brown haired man looked up then and spoke, as if he had only just become aware of her.

'There doesn't seem to be anyone underneath it,' he said as he straightened up from peering beneath the overturned vehicle. 'The driver must have managed to get out.'

'He was flung out, as it turned over,' she said breathlessly, and in that moment saw the bloodstains on the jagged rock at her feet.

Nausea welled up inside her, accompanied by a wave of faintness that made her let go of the dog and turn her back on the man as she fought against it.

'Are you all right?'

The man's voice seemed to come from a long way away from her, yet he had left the tractor and come to stand quite close to her.

'Yes,' she managed to say at last. 'It was

47

just—seeing that—' She indicated the bloodstained rock. 'I hadn't expected—I was not prepared for that.'

'Yes, it looks as if the driver was injured, but he'll be in hospital now I expect.'

'Yes, he is. He's critically injured, and he might be brain damaged.' Her voice shook, then her shoulders began to shake so badly that the man put out a hand to offer her support.

'It's someone you know? Someone close to you?' he guessed.

'My brother. My twin brother, Laurie.' She gulped back the sob that was rising in her throat.

'Oh God, I'm sorry! I had no idea—I thought the accident had just happened and that someone might be trapped. That's why I came to take a look. I was not prying, I promise you.'

'I know you weren't. The accident happened yesterday, some time in the morning I think. I suppose someone will come and move the tractor, but perhaps the police have to give permission first.' She began to shiver again and the man tried to put his hand on her shoulder but the dog growled at him. Amber spoke softly to her and she became quiet but remained watchful.

'She's my brother's dog, but she's very protective towards me too and she doesn't know you.' Amber smiled at the man, whose face was vaguely familiar to her though she could not put a name to him.

He grinned and his rugged face relaxed and became younger looking. His brown eyes filled with amusement.

'Many of the dogs around here do know me, because I'm the vet,' he explained. 'I don't think you remember me, but we have met before, though it was some time ago. Fergus Carew, from the Middleby veterinary practice.'

Memory came to her aid then. Remembrance of a day she would much rather forget. The day she had discovered Rory and Zoe together in the moorland inn where she had taken an injured puppy to await the arrival of this man.

'We met at the Moorcock Inn when young Lucky nearly met his end under your car wheels,' he reminded her.

'Yes, I remember now. Did you manage to find the owners of the puppy?'

'No. It seems he had been abandoned by them.'

'Poor thing! What did you do with him?'

'Oh, I found him a new home. I kept him myself. He's in the car right now and probably kicking up a fuss because I haven't brought him down here with me. Are you going to say hello to him?' Fergus said with a smile.

Amber smiled back. 'Yes, I'd like to, when I've got Chance into my car. She went missing this morning and I came out looking for her. I never thought of her coming back to the tractor, but I suppose she was looking for Laurie. If you hadn't stopped when you did and gone racing down the fell I might have missed her.'

'As I said, I thought the accident had just happened and I was afraid someone might be trapped.'

She was puzzled. 'I thought everyone would have known by now about it. News travels fast around here, especially bad news.'

'I only came back from my holiday in Scotland last night,' he explained.

'I came down from there yesterday too, when I heard what had happened to Laurie. I work in a small country hotel in the Highlands.'

'I wondered what had happened to you. Why I never saw you when I was over this way. Your home is at Edengate Farm, isn't it?'

'Yes, which reminds me that I must be going. I've got loads to do about the farm while Laurie is in hospital.'

She began immediately to make the steep ascent of the rocky gulley, but soon found herself outstripped by Fergus Carew. When she was forced to stop to get her breath back Fergus held out a helping hand to her, which brought another growl from Chance.

'She's going to miss Laurie dreadfully,' Amber told Fergus then as they reached the parking place.

50

'How are you going to manage on the farm? Is there anyone to help you? Any paid labour?'

'There's only Tom, my younger brother. He's fourteen. He'll do his best, but he has to go to school. He didn't go today and he says he's not going until Laurie comes out of hospital. I don't think he realizes how long that could be.' Amber sighed as she contemplated the problems ahead of her.

'Maybe I could give you a hand sometimes?' Fergus offered.

'Will you have time? I mean, isn't the veterinary practice a very busy one?'

'Yes, but I do get some time off, and I'd be glad to help.'

'Thanks, Fergus.' She smiled at him. 'I'll just say hello to the puppy then I must go.'

When she peered into the back of the estate car she saw that the puppy had grown into a fine young dog of mixed breed but with a coat of curling silky hair of a rusty auburn shade that was the same colour as that of his master. He wagged his tail at her and gave her a doggy grin.

'He wouldn't grin at me like that if he remembered that it was my car that ran into him,' she told Fergus.

'I don't know about that. Dogs are marvellous creatures in that respect, they never hold grievances against people. You did him a good turn in a way because if you hadn't run into him he might have got lost on the moors and fallen down one of the old mine shafts.'

She felt a lifting of her spirits. 'I never thought of it like that. So something good came out of that awful day after all!'

Fergus was studying her face intently as he said 'It wasn't just the accident with Lucky that upset you that day, was it? I always felt that there was something else. Something quite different.'

'Yes, there was,' she whispered. 'But it's something that is best forgotten now. Something that I have to put behind me, for my brother's sake.'

Abruptly she turned away from him and got into her car, then with a swift wave of farewell to Fergus drove as fast as she dared back to Edengate Farm.

CHAPTER FOUR

Once back at the farm, Amber set about restoring order to the neglected kitchen because she knew that after tomorrow she would not have Tom there to help with the farm work. She intended that he should go back to school then, even though he would not like it, so she must take on much of the farm work herself and catch up on the housework at weekends when Tom was at home.

All that afternoon she laboured, scrubbing

furiously at the grease-encrusted cooker, the grimy windows, worktops, shelves and sinks. Finally, when all else was done she set about scrubbing the red tiled floor. Her work was interrupted several times by phone calls from family friends and neighbours who all wanted the latest news of Laurie and to offer their sympathy.

Their concern warmed her and helped her to conquer her weariness and anxiety. They would get through this crisis, somehow, she and Tom and Laurie, she told herself as she knelt again to get on with the cleaning of the filthy floor. But she must stop herself from being afraid every time the phone rang that it would be the hospital ringing to give her bad news. As soon as this final stretch of floor was finished she was going to put the kettle on and make a large pot of tea for herself and Tom, who was at present coping with the milking. After that she would take a hot, scented bath and change her grubby jeans and sweater for something more presentable for her evening visit to Laurie.

She did not look up when the door opened behind her as she mopped up soap bubbles from the last section of floor. Instead she threw instructions crisply over her shoulder.

'Stay where you are for a minute until I spread some newspapers for you to walk on! It's taken me ages to get this floor clean. I don't know how long it is since Zoe paid any attention to it. It was absolutely filthy.'

Arching her aching back, she pulled herself upright and began to spread out old copies of the daily newspaper to absorb the fresh mud from Tom's Wellingtons. It was not until she had placed the last sheet in position, before the back door, that she became aware that the feet standing patiently on the back door step did not belong to her young brother. Tom did not wear hand made shoes of finest cream leather, or elegantly tailored high-fashion slacks of the same shade. Her gaze travelled upwards and found a pale suede casual jacket worn open over a designer sweater, then finally came to rest on a long, lean face that was deeply tanned. Above the neat dark moustache smoke grey eyes were regarding her gravely.

'Hello, Amber,' Rory said very softly.

Amber felt her throat swell ominously. It took her a long moment to come to terms with the fact that she could no longer avoid meeting Rory.

'Hello,' she muttered, dropping her gaze down to the outspread newspapers since she could not bear to see the pity in Rory's eyes.

'How are you?' he asked, with the faintest trace of awkwardness.

'How do you think?' Her dry throat made her words sound rough and almost aggressive.

'Perhaps I should have asked you how Laurie is?'

'Didn't your father tell you? His condition is
54

still critical, and there could be brain damage.'

'I haven't been home yet, so I wondered if there had been any change since Dad telephoned to give me the news. I came straight here from the airport.'

Her eyes widened as she looked past him to find out if he had brought Zoe with him. She could not see a female figure.

'Did you—are you on your own?' she managed to ask at last.

'Yes.'

'Didn't you tell Zoe? Didn't you tell her that she had to come back at once?'

Now it was his turn to drop his gaze, and to look acutely uncomfortable.

'I tried, Amber. I really did try, but I couldn't seem to make her understand how serious Laurie's condition is. She said there was no point in her coming back, and that she couldn't face it because it would upset her too much.'

'Upset her! What about Laurie?' A slow burn of anger began deep inside Amber.

Rory shrugged his slender shoulders. 'I did everything I could, said everything I could think of, to try and persuade her to come back, but she refused to believe that there was anything she could do that would help Laurie. So I decided to come back myself and see if there was anything I could do for you.'

It was guilt that had brought him back to her, she guessed. The knowledge that he had ruined her brother's marriage as well as spoiling her own life. She took a deep breath, and hoped that her voice would come out steady as she answered him.

'I'll let you know if there is anything, Rory, and thanks for coming. Now I'll have to go and have a bath and change my clothes ready to visit Laurie.'

She glanced down at her mud spattered sweater and shabby jeans. What a mess she must look, and what a contrast to Zoe, who always looked immaculate!

'Of course. I mustn't detain you.'

For a long moment she endured the compassion in his glance, then she picked up the bucket of dirty water ready to tip it down the drain in the yard. This meant that Rory was forced to move out of her way. She expected him to stride hastily away from her. Instead he stayed and faced her as she was about to re-enter the house.

'You haven't forgiven me yet, have you Amber?' he said in a low voice.

'What do you think?' She was unable to keep the bitterness out of her voice. 'When you talked Zoe into running away with you, you ruined Laurie's life. He had nothing to live for, and so he became careless about his own safety. When the accident happened he was driving the tractor in an area that he knew was very dangerous, a place my father always said was to be avoided. Yet Laurie deliberately

56

took the tractor up there. Don't you feel a bit responsible for that, Rory? You and Zoe—'

Rory listened to her in silence, while the dark colour mounted to his high cheekbones. Then he hit back.

'Surely you are not trying to blame me for the accident when I was not even there! Come off it, Amber! Laurie has been driving a tractor for long enough to know where he should, or should not, be using it.'

'Yes, when he's in his normal state of mind! But he hasn't been his normal self since Zoe left him. He's been letting things go, on the farm and in the house, Tom said. If you hadn't stolen his wife—'

'Stolen her? That's a bit strong, Amber. Zoe would have gone to Spain whether I went or not. She made no secret of that fact to either me or Laurie. Being a farmer's wife was just not her scene.'

'She should have thought of that before she married Laurie—'

'She did. In fact she had doubts after her first visit here, but Laurie persuaded her that she would get used to the life, and promised he would not object to her going on with her work. Then he started objecting whenever she wanted to be away for a day or two.'

'Only because he suspected she was making excuses about working or going to see her aunt when all the time she was meeting you.'

This time the voice came from Tom, who

57

was standing in the open doorway of the milking parlour glaring at Rory.

Rory turned to face the boy. 'If I were you, Tom, I wouldn't be getting involved in things you know little or nothing about. You are not old enough to understand—'

'I understand about you,' Tom hit back. 'Two-timing Amber when you were engaged to her, and making up to Zoe even though you knew she was Laurie's wife.'

Rory shrugged that off, and turned back to Amber. 'I'd better go. I only came here to see if I could help, but I seem to have made matters worse. I'm sorry, Amber. So sorry.'

His eyes were bleak, his mouth taut. Amber fought against the pain that engulfed her. She must not let herself feel sympathy for him. He was part of her past now, and this was no time for looking back.

'Thank you for coming. It was kind of you,' she muttered as she averted her face and stumbled past him into the farmhouse.

She must not cry, she told herself as she rushed up the stairs to her room. Instead she must concentrate all her efforts on getting herself clean and tidy ready for the journey to the hospital. Nothing mattered except that Laurie should get better, and that she and Tom kept the farm going for him. If she concentrated all her thoughts on that she would not have time to admit to herself how much it hurt to see Rory again.

Rory would not be in a hurry to come back to the farm after the way she had spoken to him today, she reflected as she lay in a steaming bath trying to soak away her weariness and grief. He was too proud to do that.

Tom's thoughts on the subject were voiced as they drank tea and ate buttered toast before leaving for the hospital.

'I hope you are not going to encourage Rory Ashton to start coming here again. Laurie won't like it,' he said with brutal frankness.

'No, of course not. I had no idea he was coming today.'

'Why did he come?' Tom asked belligerently.

'To offer us help, at least that's what he said.'

Tom scowled. 'I don't believe that. I expect he was trying to make up to you again now that Zoe's not here.' He paused, then went on, 'Is she coming back? Did he say?'

'He said she won't come back because she doesn't think she can do anything for Laurie.'

Tom gave vent to an angry exclamation. 'She's done enough! Enough to wreck Laurie's life and ours too.'

'Hush, Tom,' she urged. 'Don't upset yourself. It won't help Laurie you know.'

'Nothing will help Laurie now, will it?' The boy's eyes were full of despair.

Amber felt her own throat tighten as she listened to him. Then she got to her feet and searched her mind for words with which to give him courage.

'The doctors will help him, Tom, you'll see! He'll pull through, will Laurie. Now let's get along to the hospital and see if there's any better news.'

In spite of the brave words she had uttered for Tom's benefit Amber was full of apprehension by the time they reached the intensive care unit. There was no change in their brother's condition, and it was too soon, they were told, for the specialist who had seen him that day to be able to give them an opinion about how serious his injuries were.

'You'll need to be very patient,' the sister in charge of his case told them. 'It's going to be a long haul, for you as well as for him, but he's hanging on to life and that's a good sign.'

'Is he—is he conscious yet?' Amber asked then.

The sister shook her head. 'No, but you can go and sit with him for a time. He's not allowed any other visitors yet, except of course for his wife.'

'She's abroad,' Amber said before Tom could say anything.

'She'll no doubt come back as soon as she's able?'

Amber shook her head. 'She doesn't think she can help him if she comes. They separated a few weeks ago.'

The warm hazel eyes of the pretty dark haired sister showed sympathy when she said that. Her words were comforting.

'Well, he's got you to help him. You are twins, aren't you?'

'Yes, and we've always been very close to one another.'

'He'll need you, when he comes out of his coma.' The sister smiled, then added in her attractive Scots accent, 'Things are at their worst for you just now, but I'm sure they'll get better.'

In the days that followed Amber tried to hang on to that hope as she and Tom struggled to carry on the work of the farm between them. In order to get the milking done before Tom caught the school bus she was forced to get up while it was still dark, and she had never been at her best in the early morning. Then at the other end of the day when they came back from visiting Laurie there were things to do in the house, clothes to iron and food to prepare and rooms to clean when she was not simply too tired to stay awake any longer.

Tiredness was a great problem as one long work filled day followed another. There were things she ought to do but just could not find the energy to tackle. Things like the farm paperwork. She was going to catch up on that when she got round to it, but there were just so many other things to be done first.

Tom was feeling the strain too, and asking more and more often why he could not stay at home and do the farm work. Most nights he

61

was too weary to be able to cope with his homework and she lacked the energy to insist that he did it. Sooner or later that would bring down the wrath of his headmaster, but that was just another problem to be shelved for the time being. One or two neighbouring farmers had helped with outstanding tasks on Edengate Farm, and Amber was grateful for that, but the day to day running of the place had to be done by Amber and Tom.

'It's stupid me going to school when so many things need doing on the farm,' Tom said one morning when she reminded him it was time he finished his breakfast and went for the school bus. 'There's fencing to be mended up on Middle Fell or the sheep will be getting onto the road.'

'I know, you told me last week, and I've been wondering what we could do about it ever since,' she said with a frown.

'You could get one of the local firms to do it, but it would be cheaper to let me stay off school.' Tom grinned as he crammed the last piece of toast into his mouth and prepared to make a last minute dash for the bus.

'No, Tom! I'll find some way to get it done.'

When he had gone she let her mind worry round this latest problem while she washed the breakfast dishes. There was no question of them being able to pay anyone to repair the broken fences on Middle Fell because when the latest bank statement had arrived a day or so ago she had been shocked to discover that there was not enough money available to do any more than pay the outstanding accounts for farm supplies. She was still worrying about this when she heard a vehicle come to a halt in the yard. A glance through the kitchen window and a glimpse of the now familiar estate car belonging to Fergus Carew gave her spirits a lift. She hurried to the door.

'Fergus, it's good to see you! Have you time for a coffee?' she greeted him.

'Yes, for once I'm ahead of my schedule.' Fergus followed her into the kitchen after stopping to exchange greetings with the two dogs.

'How are you managing?' he asked as he dropped into one of the chairs that were set about the kitchen table.

'With some difficulty, there are a lot more problems than I expected. I just hadn't realized—' She sighed and broke off there.

'Why not sit down and tell me about your problems? Maybe then we'll find some ways in which I can help you.'

Suddenly then she longed to share with this nice, uncomplicated man the immense burden of worries that her brother's accident had thrown on to her unprepared shoulders. She made the coffee then placed the two mugs on the table and sat opposite him. Fergus had telephoned her a couple of days after their meeting at the scene of the accident to ask for news of her brother, and later he had called in on his way from a visit to the livery stables on the other side of the village. He had not stayed long, but dropped in again a day or two later. On both these occasions she had been reluctant to share her anxieties about the farm with him but now she was desperately in need of someone to talk to, and she had a feeling that Fergus, who spent much of his working life among farmers, would be the one to understand.

'I don't know where to begin,' she confessed, after sipping her coffee then clenching her hands around the mug.

'Your brother is no worse, is he?'

'No. His condition is stable, though he's still unconscious.'

'So?'

'My main worry is about how to get the fences mended on Middle Fell before we lose any sheep. You see we can't afford to pay anyone to do that sort of work because with farm prices down there just isn't enough money coming in to do anything more than pay the bills that we already owe. Tom wants me to let him stay away from school to do the job, but apart from the fact that I don't think he's strong enough I also don't want him to be in trouble for skipping school.'

'He could probably manage to do the job at the weekend if he had some help,' Fergus suggested. 'I'm not on call this Saturday, so I could come and give him a hand.'

'Oh, would you? I'd be so grateful Fergus, if you are sure you don't have anything else planned for your day off. What do you usually do?'

'Go fell walking, or if the weather isn't right for that I go to a film or a play in Darlington or Durham.'

'You're sure you won't have to alter any arrangements you've already made with friends, or anything?'

'Absolutely. I've been rather a loner since I came here because James, my senior partner, was not well when I first came so I spent most of my time working and didn't have much time for making friends.'

'Then you're not married, or anything? I wouldn't like to upset—'

'No, I'm not married, or anything!' he laughed. 'I nearly was, a couple of years ago, but I'll tell you about that another time.' He changed the subject then by asking her for how long she would be able to stay away from her job in Scotland.

'I'll be staying here for as long as I'm needed, and I don't know just how long that will be. I only know that it will be a long time before Laurie is fit enough to come home, and that I can't leave Tom to manage on his own. There's no-one else to look after him, now that Laurie's wife has left him.'

'That must have made things much harder

65

for you. I suppose there's no chance of her coming back?'

'I asked her to come back, for Laurie's sake, but she refused. So I'll have to stay.'

'Which means you might lose your job in Scotland, if they can't wait for you?'

She nodded. 'They'll be busy soon with the Christmas dinners and parties, so I suppose I'll have to write and tell them I won't be going back.'

'Why did you go so far away to work, when you are so devoted to your brothers?' Fergus wanted to know.

Amber hesitated, then decided to tell him the truth.

'It was because of Zoe, Laurie's wife. Because I discovered she had been meeting someone else while she was supposed to be visiting an elderly aunt who is in a nursing home.'

Fergus frowned. 'I'm not sure I quite understand why you felt you had to go, Amber. I mean, if you saw your brother's marriage was breaking up wouldn't that make you think he might need your help?'

She traced a pattern on the table with her finger while she gathered her courage to tell him the rest.

'I hardly thought about what was going to happen to Laurie,' she confessed. 'I was too busy thinking about my own misery and trying to escape from it. You see the man Zoe was meeting was the man I was planning to marry the following spring. When I discovered that Rory was deceiving me I couldn't bear to stay here, with him living so close. I knew we would be certain to keep meeting if I stayed, so I took the job in Scotland.'

'It must have been very hard for you to come back,' he said quietly.

'Yes.'

'Was it Rory Ashton you were engaged to, Amber?'

'Yes. Do you know him?'

'Slightly, through my work. He must be feeling very bad about what happened to your brother.'

Amber shrugged. 'I suppose he does. He came to offer help as soon as he heard about the accident. Came back from Spain, in fact. Though he couldn't persuade Zoe to come. I wouldn't accept any help from him, I was too angry and upset because I blamed him as much as Zoe for what happened.'

Fergus stared at her. 'For the accident, you mean? Why should you do that?'

'Because after Zoe left to go to Spain with Rory, Laurie just lost heart about everything. According to Tom, he became very careless about his own safety. He knew it was not safe to take a tractor up on to Top Moor, yet he did so and now—'

Her final words were lost as the ringing of the telephone broke into them. Her heart seemed to stop when she heard Sister Campbell speaking to her from the hospital.

'Yes, it is Amber Wakefield speaking,' she forced herself to respond.

'I have good news for you,' the soft Scottish voice told her. 'Your brother has regained consciousness.'

'Really?' Amber whispered.

'Yes, really! You'll see for yourself, if you'd like to come along.'

'Yes, yes I'll do that right away! Thank you, sister.'

As Amber went back to share the news with Fergus the tears of joy were already beginning to slide down her cheeks. Fergus saw the tears and misunderstood them. He opened his arms and drew her close so that she could weep against his shoulder.

CHAPTER FIVE

'What is it, Amber?' Fergus asked as she struggled to regain her composure. 'Not bad news, I hope?'

'No! No! It's very good news, Fergus. The best! Laurie is conscious at last, and Sister Campbell says I can go in to see him at once.'

His strong, square, freckled face lit up with the delight he caught from her. 'That's wonderful. I'm very glad for you.' He looked into her face, where tears were drying on the thick brown lashes as a smile deepened the blue of her eyes. 'You should smile more often, you look so lovely when you are happy.'

She laughed, and while her mouth was still quivering he began to kiss her. Taken by surprise, she did not pull away from him but accepted the kiss, even enjoyed it. Then she laughed again, rather shakily, and said 'Thanks, Fergus, but I must go. I can't wait to get to the hospital; to actually talk to Laurie.'

Fergus's warm brown eyes became grave as he offered her tentative words of warning. 'Don't expect too much, as yet, darling.'

'What do you mean?'

He hesitated, then said 'I mean don't expect to find your brother back to normal yet. That might take some time.'

She sobered. 'Yes, I know what you are trying to say, but at least I can begin to hope now that he will be well again one day. Thanks for trying to help, Fergus, I do appreciate it.'

Already she was reaching for her handbag and her car keys, eager to be on her way to the hospital.

'I must be off now. I'll see you on Saturday, if not before.'

He left her then to continue with his round of visits. Amber followed him out into the yard and started up her car engine, full of excitement at the thought of being able to talk to Laurie at last, full of hope for the future for the first time since her arrival back at Edenby.

Sister Campbell was waiting to speak to her when she reached the hospital, her calm, beautiful face full of her pleasure at being able to give better news of her patient at last.

'I thought it wouldn't take you long to get here, once you heard the good news. Don't make it too long a visit this time though, will you, because Mr Richards is coming in to see him soon. You can come again tonight, if you wish, and your young brother too.'

'Oh yes, Tom will want to come. He'll be so excited when I tell him.'

At first when Amber reached Laurie's bedside his eyes were closed and he seemed to be sleeping. Disappointment filled her, then as she took his hand and squeezed it she felt him respond and his eyes opened.

'Amber,' he whispered. 'I knew you'd come.'

She raised questioning eyes to Sister Campbell, who gave a warning shake of her head. So Laurie evidently had no idea of how many days he had been lying unconscious, and no knowledge of how many times she and Tom had visited him. Her throat tightened.

'Everything's going to be fine, Laurie,' she murmured.

'I know.' The words were uttered very slowly, as if they cost him an immense effort. 'I knew when I heard the sheep, and Chance.'

His eyes closed again then, his hand relaxed in her own. At first she was alarmed, then she

70

saw that Sister Campbell was smiling and she knew that Laurie was asleep.

'What did he mean, about hearing the sheep, and Chance, his dog?' she asked. 'You can't hear any animals when you are in here. Is he delirious?'

The sister's lovely smile deepened. 'No, Laurie isn't delirious. He did hear sheep, and a sheepdog barking. My father is a farmer up in the Borders so I asked him to record a tape of some of his sheep and his dog and send it to me so I could play it to Laurie. Sometimes familiar sounds help a patient to come out of a coma, and it worked with Laurie.'

'What was the first thing he said?' Amber wanted to know.

The other girl looked perplexed. 'He said something about a chance, of course the words were not very plain.'

'Chance is the name of his dog, his working collie,' Amber explained.

Linda Campbell laughed softly. 'Oh, I see now what he was trying to say. It was after the dog barked on the tape. I was puzzled because I've never heard of a dog being called Chance before.'

'We have two working dogs at Edengate, Chance and Risky,' Amber told her. 'Chance belongs to Laurie and Risky to Tom. Laurie had just lost an older dog he'd done well with in the sheepdog trials when a neighbouring farmer offered him this one. She was small, but

71

he decided to take a chance on her, so I suggested he name her Chance. Risky was one of her puppies, the weakling of the litter, the one nobody wanted. Tom was set on keeping him, so Laurie called him Risky. He's made a good dog too.'

'The dogs will miss your brother, especially Chance,' the sister said thoughtfully.

'Yes. Chance disappeared on the morning after the accident and when I went out looking for her I found she had gone back to where the tractor had overturned. She was just sitting there waiting for Laurie to come back, and of course standing guard over the tractor. She's very loyal to him, she wouldn't let the vet get near when he stopped because he thought the accident had just happened. If only people were as loyal,' Amber finished sadly.

'Some people are,' the sister said gently. Then 'Is there any news of your sister-in-law yet? You said you were trying to get in touch with her, but she was abroad.'

Amber sighed. 'We got a message to her, telling her about the accident, but she seemed to think there was nothing she could do if she came back.'

'Didn't she think about how he might feel,' the sister said in a low voice. 'That her being here might help his recovery?'

'Evidently not.' Amber could not keep the bitterness from her voice.

'Yet they can't have been married long—

I'm sorry, I shouldn't have said that, it was none of my business.' Now the sister looked embarrassed at her own clumsiness.

'They shouldn't have married at all. She was totally wrong for him, but he couldn't see it because he was so besotted with her. Now she's ruined all our lives,' Amber muttered under her breath.

'I'm sorry. So sorry,' the other girl said.

The sympathy in her voice brought a grain of comfort to Amber so that impulsively she gave her a quick hug and said 'You've been so good to Laurie and me. Just talking to you has helped me a lot.'

'I'm glad. I must go now because Mr Richards will be here to see Laurie very soon. I'll see you later.'

With that, Linda Campbell hurried away. She seemed really upset that Laurie's wife had not come rushing to his side, Amber mused as she sat down again beside her brother, so she must think it important to his recovery. Amber felt her heart swell with love and pity for her twin as she gazed at the still figure in the neat hospital bed. Although he was sleeping now and no longer in a coma she knew that Laurie would still have a long hard fight ahead of him. Sister Campbell had been honest with her about that. Well, she would fight for Laurie's life too, even if it meant humbling herself by making a direct appeal to Zoe to come back and see him.

Later, after she had been banished from the hospital so that Mr Richards could subject Laurie to more tests, she did some shopping in the local open market then drove home to the farm with her mind full of determination to get in touch with Zoe herself, without delay. Because to delay would be to risk losing the courage she had managed to build up since Laurie became conscious again.

She did not need to look up the telephone number she needed. It was engraved on her mind still from those long ago happier days when Rory had still been in love with her and always glad to hear her voice. As she dialled the number then waited for the ringing on the other end of the line to be answered she could feel her stomach muscles knotting with tension. Then Rory's deep voice was speaking to her.

'Edengate Hotel.'

'It's Amber, Rory.' She made herself speak very slowly and clearly so as not to betray her nervousness. 'I wondered if you could let me have Zoe's phone number?'

Rory seemed to hesitate for a long moment before answering her.

'Yes. She's back in England again now and working in London.' There was a pause then he said 'I hope Laurie is no worse?'

'No. As a matter of fact he regained consciousness this morning, though he has a long way to go still before he's well again.'

'I'm so glad it's better news. As I said before, if there's anything I can do to help you I'll be only too pleased—'

'There isn't—' she broke in. 'Except for giving me that phone number.'

'Would you like me to speak to Zoe for you? To give her the latest news of Laurie and see if she'll change her mind,' he said.

'No. It didn't do any good last time you asked her, so why should it this time? Perhaps you didn't put enough pressure on her to come back? Maybe you didn't want her to?'

The last few words were uttered before Amber could stop herself from voicing them. It was as if they had been inside her, waiting to be said, ever since she had arrived home and contacted Rory's father to ask for Zoe's address. She heard Rory's gasp of indignation and felt his anger scorch her heart as words of denial came pouring out of him.

'Just what sort of person do you think I am, Amber? You should know me better than that—'

'I thought I did, but I was wrong—'

'No, you were not,' he interrupted. 'I'm still your friend, still Laurie's friend, and I want to see him get well again. In spite of what you think of me, I did try to persuade Zoe to come back to Laurie. I never wanted her to leave him in the first place, only to go away and think things over. You've got to believe that, Amber!'

75

How could she believe it, after all the deceit that had gone before, all the lying and the hurt? She bit back the angry retort that was already trembling on her tongue and made herself answer Rory calmly.

'I don't see that it matters all that much now what I believe.'

'It matters to me, Amber. It matters a great deal,' he broke in.

If only she could believe him. It would be so wonderful to be able to trust Rory again. She missed the friendship which had existed between Laurie, Rory and herself ever since the Ashtons had come to take over the Edengate Hotel when she and Laurie were still at school. She had begun to love Rory in those days, she thought sadly, then forced her thoughts back to the present.

'You haven't given me Zoe's number yet,' she reminded him. 'I can't wait all day for it. I have things to do on the farm and in the house. So many things that I can hardly cope with them all.'

'Yet you won't accept help from me—'

'You can help me most by just giving me Zoe's phone number.'

She heard his long sigh of exasperation, then as she was about to speak again he beat her to it.

'If I get Zoe to come back and see Laurie, will you believe that I want to help you?'

'Yes,' she agreed reluctantly, 'but I don't

76

suppose a phone call from you will do any more good than one from me.'

'I'm not talking about a phone call, Amber, I'm talking about going down to London and bringing Zoe back with me.'

'If she'll come!'

'She'll come. I'll see that she does,' he said briskly.

'I'll leave it to you then, and thanks, Rory,' Amber murmured as she ended the call.

Would Rory really go down to London and persuade Zoe to come back with him, she found herself wondering as she set about preparing an evening meal that could be left to cook while she tackled some of the outstanding jobs about the farm. She hadn't collected the eggs yet because of that call from Sister Campbell and her excited dash to the hospital. Was it true, what Rory had said, that he had not wanted Zoe to leave Laurie, only to go away for a while and think things over? If only she knew.

What did it matter now, anyway, when Laurie's marriage was over and his wife would not even come and visit him when he was so dangerously ill? Amber did not think Zoe would come now, in spite of Rory's assurance that he would make her, but at least she knew she had done her best to get Zoe back.

When Tom came home from school and heard that Laurie was out of his coma at last he wanted to go at once to the hospital to see him.

77

Amber had some difficulty in persuading him that the evening milking and the eating of the chicken casserole which was now filling the farmhouse kitchen with a delicious aroma must come first.

'It's great news! Really, really great!' Tom shouted with joy. 'It won't be long before Laurie's home now.'

Amber hated having to warn him that their brother still had a long, hard fight ahead of him but she knew she must do so.

'We mustn't get too excited, Tom,' she warned. 'Laurie has a long way to go still. We don't know yet if he'll ever fully recover. If he'll be able to work the farm again, or even walk again.'

'What did he say when he came round and saw you?'

'He just said "Hello, I knew you'd come." He doesn't know how many times we've been to see him already, or how long he's been in the hospital. It was the tape that Sister Campbell asked her father to make of sheep sounds and a sheepdog barking that finally got through to him,' Amber explained.

'Why didn't we think of doing that, making a tape of our sheep and Chance? Why didn't they tell us to do that?' Tom wanted to know.

'Perhaps it was because they were not sure of whether the tape would bring him back to consciousness, and they didn't want to disappoint us.'

'It's great news, anyway. Just great!'

Her young brother's joy made Amber smile. It had been so hard, coping with his moodiness and his constant pleading to be allowed to miss school so that he could do the farm work, but he would take notice of what Laurie said, and at last Laurie would be able to talk to Tom about the farm.

When they reached his bedside that evening Laurie asked almost at once when Zoe was coming to see him. Tom and Amber exchanged glances of dismay.

'She'll come as soon as she can,' Amber said quickly, before Tom could say anything.

'I thought she would have been the first here,' Laurie whispered, forming each word with difficulty and frowning with the effort this cost him.

'Oh, but she's not—' Tom began, then stopped.

'She's been delayed,' Amber broke in.

Laurie's frown deepened. 'Don't understand—' he muttered.

Comprehension came to Amber then. Laurie did not remember that his wife had left him a few weeks before the accident. Her stomach lurched with fear. She must talk to Sister Campbell at once, or to the doctor, and find out how to cope with this new and unexpected turn of events. Only that would mean leaving Tom alone with Laurie, and suppose Tom unwittingly told their brother the truth about his wife's departure? With a surge of relief, she saw that Laurie had drifted into sleep again.

'I'm going to have a word with Sister, Tom, while Laurie is asleep. If he wakes, watch what you say to him, won't you?'

'What do you mean?' he whispered urgently.

'I mean I don't think he can remember what happened between him and Zoe.'

She took her fears to Linda Campbell, and had them confirmed.

'Yes, you are right, he is suffering from partial loss of memory. He may even remember the accident happening but have no memory of the days immediately before it.'

'What can I do to help him? How can I answer his questions without upsetting him?' Amber wanted to know.

'Isn't there any possibility of getting his wife here? It might help.'

'I'm still trying. A friend said he would go down to London and try to get her to come back with him, but he won't be able to force her to come, will he?' Amber worried.

'No,' Linda Campbell agreed. 'We can only hope she'll put Laurie first at this time, whatever their differences have been.'

'If anyone can get her here it will be Rory. She wouldn't come when I asked her to.' Amber could not keep the resentment she felt towards Zoe out of her voice.

The other girl looked at her with sympathy,

then put a hand on her shoulder and said 'Try to forget what happened, if you can, for your brother's sake. He's going to need all the support you can give him in the days to come, even if that means forgetting how you feel about your sister-in-law.'

Amber sighed. 'It's not going to be easy, under the circumstances.'

Linda Campbell nodded. 'I know how hard it must be for you, and how tired and worried you must be. Why don't you and Tom go home now and try to get some rest? You'll sleep easier now you know Laurie has taken the first step towards recovery.'

'There's work to do on the farm before we can think about sleep. I never seem to be able to catch up on all there is to do. I'll have to tackle some of the paper work tonight because it's just piling up on me.'

'Don't you have anyone who can help you, apart from Tom?' the young nursing sister asked.

Amber sighed. 'Some of our neighbours have helped where they could, but they all have their own farms to run, and we can't afford any paid help because Laurie spent quite a lot on doing up the farmhouse for Zoe when he married her. Our vet has been very good though and offered to help Tom repair some fences.'

The thought of Fergus and the help he had so readily offered warmed her thoughts as she went to tell Tom that Sister Campbell thought they should go home and get some rest. Tom was relieved, he was falling asleep at Laurie's bedside as the long days of farm work on top of school work caught up on him. He rubbed the sleep from his eyes, stretched himself and followed Amber thankfully out of the too warm atmosphere of the hospital and into the bracing fresh air of the hospital car park. He was silent at first as Amber began to drive back to Edenby, then he began to voice his doubts and fears to her.

'What are we going to do if Laurie asks us again tomorrow where Zoe is? We can't keep on lying to him, can we?'

'Yes, we can if we have to. I mean, he so obviously has no memory of Zoe leaving him before the accident that we'll just have to go along with what he believes and keep making excuses for her until she comes back. If she ever comes back,' Amber told him.

'Do you think she might come back, now Laurie is conscious again?' he wanted to know.

'I don't know. Rory says he knows where she is and will go to London to bring her back.'

'You've seen him then?' He gave her a sharp glance, then looked away again.

'I've spoken to him on the phone and asked for Zoe's phone number. He said he would go down there and see that she came back.'

'What if she won't come?'

'We'll face that when we have to, and try not

to think about it in the meantime. We have plenty of other things to think about, haven't we? All the work that needs doing on the farm. Which reminds me that Fergus Carew is going to help us repair the fences on Middle Fell next Saturday.'

'That's great! Can I work up there with him?'

Amber smiled at his enthusiasm. 'Yes, when the milking and foddering up is done.'

Tom yawned widely and noisily. She glanced at him with concern and saw that he was already drifting into sleep again. He looked worn out, and there was his homework still to be done before he went to bed. She was very tired herself, having been on the go since early that morning, and she longed for an early night but it was time to bring the farm books up to date for the VAT inspector so she would have to give that task top priority or there would be another problem facing her.

When Tom had long been in bed and it was past midnight, she realized that she must have nodded off herself because the pen she had been using for the form filling had fallen from her hand and she had slid down in her chair. Something had woken her, bringing her to instant awareness. Maybe the dogs barking out in the yard to signal that there was a fox about. She tensed her body as the door behind her opened, and turned slowly to face Rory.

'Oh, it's you!' She let out a long sigh. 'I must have fallen asleep, and you startled me.' What was Rory doing here at this time of night, she wondered uneasily. 'I thought you had gone to London?'

'Yes, I did go to London,' he said quietly.

'If you are back already, I suppose Zoe wouldn't come?' she guessed.

'Oh yes, she's here.'

Amber rose stiffly to her feet and stared past him, looking beyond his tall figure for the slight form of her sister-in-law and not finding it.

'She's at the hotel,' he explained. 'I thought that was the best place for her, in the circumstances. We have plenty of empty rooms at this time of the year.'

Something was still puzzling Amber. 'How did you get in? I didn't hear you.'

'Through the back door. I did knock, though not very loudly as I guessed Tom would be in bed and I didn't want to disturb him.'

'I must have forgotten to lock the door because I was in such a hurry to get the VAT returns done. Then I went and fell asleep over them,' she confessed.

'I'm not surprised. You look worn out. Why don't you go to bed and leave me to do them for you?'

Amber stared at him. 'What about Zoe? Won't she be waiting for you?'

He laughed dryly. 'I doubt it! In fact she's not very pleased with me at the moment for dragging her up here when she would much

84

rather have stayed down in London. My father said he would see her settled in while I came to tell you she was here.'

Amber was perplexed about that. 'You could have just telephoned me. You must be tired if you've driven to London and back in a day?'

'I managed to get a couple of hours sleep while I waited for Zoe to finish the modelling job she was involved with when I arrived, and I didn't phone you because I thought a telephone call so late at night while Laurie was so ill might alarm you.'

She felt foolish tears of utter weariness threaten to escape when she heard that. 'Oh Rory, that was very thoughtful of you. I don't know what to say—' Her voice broke and she turned away from him so that he should not see how overcome with emotion she was. It was too late for that though, he had seen her face crumple and was moving closer to take her into his arms.

'I'd do more than that for you, darling, so much more if only you would let me.'

Her mouth trembled beneath the pressure of his long kiss and she allowed herself to relax against him. It was so comforting to be held in this way, to feel the warmth of him, the familiar strength of his body, as all the tensions of the recent stressful days ebbed away and left her feeling that nothing mattered except this moment.

Then the kisses were becoming more ardent, the caressing hands more urgent. It would be so easy now to let herself believe that there had been no Zoe, no deception, no violent row and no parting from him. Yet she could not quite quell the voice deep inside her that wanted to ask questions, and wanted those questions to be answered before it was too late and she had committed herself again to Rory.

'What about Zoe?' she made herself ask.

His hold on her tightened as he said 'That's over. I think it really ended when she wouldn't come and see Laurie when I first asked her. When he was still critically ill. It opened my eyes to what she was really like, I think. Before that I was kind of bewitched by her beauty and charm. I fought against it right from the beginning, but Zoe made it harder for me by seeking my company. I'm not proud of what happened, Amber. In fact I feel ashamed of the way I deceived both you and Laurie, but I seemed to be unable to help myself. As I said, I was bewitched by her. Do you understand what I'm trying to say?'

Rory was telling her that his enchantment with her brother's wife was over and that he had come to his senses again and wanted her to resume their old relationship. She ought to be overjoyed, thrilled and excited, but strangely she was not. There was just a numbness inside her, and an unutterable tiredness that seemed to be clouding her judgement.

'Do you understand?' he repeated.

'Yes, I think so.'

'How do you feel about it?'

'I don't know, Rory. I just don't know. Perhaps it's too soon to ask me.'

Maybe something had gone from their relationship never to return, along with the complete trust she had once known with him. All she felt now was confusion and uncertainty, and fear of what the future might bring.

'Things are so different now, Rory. There's Laurie to be considered, and Tom. While they both need me so much there's no point in considering my own feelings, and I'm so tired—'

Instantly then Rory was contrite. 'What a fool I am darling, to expect you to make decisions when you are exhausted. Go to bed now and we'll talk tomorrow when you are able to think straight.'

He kissed her gently and with his arm about her shoulders urged her out of the kitchen and to the foot of the staircase. Her heart began to beat more rapidly then. Was he expecting her, in spite of what she had just said to him, to slip easily back into the sort of relationship they had once enjoyed?

She was aware of a great surge of relief washing over her as he said softly 'Goodnight, Amber darling. Sleep well!' before turning away from her and going back into the kitchen.

CHAPTER SIX

Almost as soon as her head hit the pillow Amber fell into a deep sleep from which she did not emerge until the shrill summons of the radio alarm which she had borrowed from Laurie's room brought her back from her slumbers. Instantly then she was wide awake and sliding out from beneath the duvet to reach for her dressing robe. Stretching herself and shivering a little in the damp early morning air she drew back her curtains to take a look at the weather, and saw through the thick mist that swirled about the farmhouse and the yard the long, sleek, silver shape of Rory's car illuminated by the outside light which she had forgotten to switch off last night.

Surely Rory was not still here at the farm? Surely he would have gone back to the hotel, once she had decided to go to bed? So why was his car still here? As the questions crowded into her mind her bare feet were already crossing her bedroom at speed and from there racing down the stairs that led into the back hall.

When she reached the last step she paused to tie the sash of her brilliantly coloured silk dressing robe. She was puzzled then by the silence that was all about her. If Rory had come back to the farm for some reason early this morning why wasn't he talking to Tom,

88

since Tom was usually up and about by now?

Frowning, she pushed open the kitchen door. Then she halted in astonishment at the sight that awaited her. In the big old Windsor chair which had belonged to Grandfather Wakefield was Rory, soundly asleep and looking completely relaxed and comfortable with his head resting on an ancient crocheted cushion. Zoe had banished that chair to one of the farm buildings when she had ordered the refurbishing of the kitchen, Amber recalled. Evidently after her departure either Laurie or Tom had brought it back.

Smiling to herself at the picture Rory presented in his elegant expensive clothes, with his hair awry and a dark growth of stubble on his chin, Amber crossed the room to fill the kettle and set it to boil, then frowned again as she tried to fathom out why Rory was still here instead of down at the family hotel where he lived and worked. Why wasn't he at the Edengate Hotel? Especially now that Zoe was there.

Could it be true, what he had tried to convince her of last night, that his affair with Zoe was over and he regretted that it had ever begun? Could she believe that? Did she want to believe it, or would she rather go on believing that Rory was not to be trusted?

With her mind in a turmoil, she poured boiling water into the teapot and reached down mugs from one of the cupboards. It would be safer to think of Rory as part of her past, no matter how hard he tried to convince her otherwise, then she would not be hurt again she decided as she filled three mugs with the hot, strong brew before going to give Rory's shoulder a firm shake.

'Wake up, Rory,' she urged.

Slowly his eyes flickered open and came to rest on her face. Slowly, lazily, he smiled up at her as he said 'Good morning, Amber darling!'

She moved away from him as his gaze travelled from her eyes to the rest of her, clad in the clinging silk robe.

'The sight of you makes a good start to my day,' he murmured as he reached for her with both hands.

Amber took a step backwards and put her question. 'What are you doing here? Why aren't you at the hotel?'

'Because I stayed here and did your VAT returns, as I said I would, then tiredness caught up on me and I just couldn't keep my eyes open. I decided to have a few minutes with my eyes closed before driving home, so I wouldn't fall asleep at the wheel, and I suppose I've slept ever since.'

'You must have been very uncomfortable, very cramped, in that chair,' she commented.

He grinned at her. 'I did consider an alternative, but I thought you might not appreciate my company in the state of exhaustion you were suffering from last night.'

90

That made her cheeks burn. 'I've made some tea,' she said crisply, 'but I can't ask you to stay to breakfast because there's too much to do here in the mornings before I get Tom off to school. In any case, you'll want to get back to the hotel to see how Zoe is, won't you?' she added as she moved even further away from him.

Rory drained the mug she had placed beside him and got to his feet, stretching his tall, slender body upright with the same easy grace that he gave to all his movements.

'You don't believe what I told you last night, do you Amber?'

'I can't honestly remember just what you said to me last night,' she lied. 'All I can remember is how tired I was.'

He took a couple of steps towards her before he spoke again and said 'I suppose I only have myself to blame for you not choosing to remember, but I did mean what I said about being sorry for the pain I caused you, and I really do still love you. You have to believe that.'

Before she realized what he intended, he was across the room in a couple of swift strides and catching her in his arms to strain her to him so tightly that she was unable to breathe, and unable to escape from the flame that spread from his body to her own. For a few mad seconds everything fled from her mind except that burning desire; nothing else mattered but this powerful attraction that flared as suddenly between them as it had done in the early days of their love affair before Zoe entered their lives and drove them apart.

'Now do you believe me?' he whispered as his lips fought to silence her doubts.

Her whole being longed to give in to his pleading, to respond to the promise of delight that his long embrace offered, but the moment of choice was shattered as Tom bounded noisily down the stairs and into the room before they had time to draw apart.

'Oh, it's you!' Tom's voice was curt and the glance he shot at Rory was full of hostility.

Embarrassment flooded Amber as she attempted to struggle free of Rory's embrace, and to pull together the thin silk of her dressing robe. She was aware all the time of the amused gleam in Rory's eyes as she struggled to regain her self possession.

'Yes, it's me Tom,' Rory said coolly. 'I arrived very late last night, while you were in bed, to tell Amber that I had managed to bring Zoe back with me. She was falling asleep over the VAT returns so I stayed on to finish them for her, and fell asleep myself in this chair.'

Tom's frown deepened. 'So Zoe's back in this house! I wonder how long for?'

'Not in this house, Tom,' Rory corrected him. 'I thought it would be easier for all of you if she stayed at the hotel for the time being.'

'And easier for you, of course,' Tom chipped

in tartly.

Amber turned her back on both of them and went to pick up the teapot from the top of the Aga and pour tea into a big mug for her brother.

'There's no need for you to take that attitude, Tom,' she heard Rory say sternly. 'As I've explained to Amber, that episode is over and I deeply regret that it ever began since the last thing I ever wanted was to hurt either Amber or Laurie.'

'It's easy for you to say that now, when the damage is done!' her brother broke in, his voice charged with emotion. 'It's not you—lying there in the hospital hardly able to move or speak, but it ought to have been you!'

'Surely you are not trying to blame me for the accident, Tom?'

Rory's voice was so quiet, so unemotional, but his eyes were appalled, Amber saw as she turned her gaze from Tom to him.

'Well, if it was anyone's fault it was yours and Zoe's, because after you went away together Laurie just didn't care any more what happened to him or to the farm or to me. He knew it was dangerous to take a tractor up on Top Moor, he always told me it was, yet he went up there himself that day in bad weather conditions when it was more dangerous than ever. He did it because he didn't care any more what happened to him,' Tom repeated. His voice broke as he came to the end of

93

the accusation.

Rory's face became haggard as he listened to the boy piling the blame for Laurie's accident on to him. He turned his stricken gaze on to Amber, wondering whether she would come to his defence, and recognized the same expression of condemnation.

'What can I say?' Rory's shoulders sagged as he allowed a long sigh of defeat to escape him. 'What can I say that will convince either of you that I would not have brought such disaster to Laurie if I could possibly have helped it?' Then, speaking with a hesitation that was quite foreign to his usual self confident style, he went on 'I suppose one can't hope that anyone as immature as Tom will try to understand, but I had felt that you, Amber, might have known that I never intended any harm to come to any of you because of my friendship with Zoe.'

'No harm would have come to any of us if it had just been friendship between you and Zoe. She wouldn't have run away with you if you had only been friends, would she?' Amber felt bound to point out to him.

'She didn't run away with me! It wasn't like that,' he retaliated. 'I had arranged to go and stay with friends who have a hotel in Spain, at the end of our tourist season. I suppose I must have talked about the place to Zoe but I certainly didn't expect to find her already staying there when I arrived.'

An exclamation of disbelief came from Tom.

94

Amber remained silent while she wondered how much of this was true; how much invented to save face for Rory.

'When I asked Zoe what she was doing there she said she had just felt desperate to get away to somewhere she could think things over and decide what to do for the best, for both her and Laurie.'

'But you didn't tell her to come back here and sort it out with Laurie, did you?' Amber found herself voicing that thought as soon as it came into her mind.

Rory smiled faintly at the absurdity of that suggestion. 'Do you imagine, knowing your sister-in-law, that she would have been likely to listen to that advice?'

He had a point there, she knew. Right from her arrival at the farm for the first time Zoe had done what she wanted to do, made what changes she wanted without consulting anyone else. Yet still Amber was unwilling to admit that Rory could be right and Zoe would not listen to anything he had to say, unless it suited her. The whole discussion about Zoe and Rory and that hotel in Spain was proving to be upsetting to her, and she was determined to bring it to an end.

'There's no point in going over all that now. We are just wasting time and right now I can't afford to do that. I'm going to get dressed so I can make your breakfast Tom, so will you get on with the milking, please?'

With a clatter, Tom put down his empty mug and made for the door that led into the yard. Amber heard the two dogs welcome him, then Rory spoke to her again and she remembered that she had not thanked him for the work he had done on the farm books.

'Thanks for your help, Rory,' she began awkwardly. 'With the VAT, and—and with getting Zoe back.'

'You're welcome,' he told her. 'I know I've got it right with the paperwork, I'm very used to that, but I'm not so sure about Zoe. How it will work out, I mean. Whether it will help Laurie—'

Amber sighed, sharing his uncertainty, feeling afraid of the future. 'Time will tell. Thanks again. I'll be seeing you!' This last remark was thrown over her shoulder as she hurried into the hall to go up to her room and dress.

'I hope so,' came Rory's reply.

She heard the door of his car slam shut as she raced upstairs, heard the powerful engine roar into life and watched from her window as he steered the long car through the open farm gate and turned it left down the long hill that led to the village and the Edengate Hotel, and to Zoe. Then she turned away from the window, determined not to let her thoughts dwell on him any more but to give all her concentration to the task of keeping the farm going for Laurie. Because it was Laurie who mattered most to her now, not Rory Ashton.

It was easy enough for her to keep this resolution in the frantic rush of helping Tom to finish the morning milking, cooking him a substantial breakfast, gathering the eggs, taking delivery of a load of animal feed which was required for the winter months, and sharing a quick coffee with the delivery man while she answered his enquiries about her brother's progress. Not so easy though to keep her thoughts away from Rory, and whether she could believe him, when she was alone in the farmhouse kitchen preparing vegetables for the chicken casserole which was to provide an evening meal for her and Tom. She was relieved when the barking of the collies gave warning that a stranger was entering the yard, but the feeling evaporated swiftly when she recognized Rory's car.

Was he going to make her life even more difficult than it already was by coming to the farm at every opportunity? Her heart began to hammer against her ribs, because now she was alone here and vulnerable, with no Tom to interrupt a too-emotive scene and save her from becoming involved again with a man she was not sure she could trust.

The door of the sleek silver car was opening. She held her breath, then let it out on a long sigh as she saw a petite female figure emerge from the vehicle. Zoe was here.

She had known that this moment must

come, but she still felt quite unprepared for it. Chance and Risky continued to bark, drowning the sound of Zoe's spiky heels as she advanced over the concrete to the back door and stood there hesitating; wondering whether to knock and wait to be admitted now that she no longer lived here. Or to knock and walk in, as friends and neighbours would.

'So you've come,' Amber said quietly as she held open the heavy door and surveyed her sister-in-law coolly.

'Yes. I arrived last night.'

Did that mean that Zoe was not aware that Rory had come to tell Amber of her arrival at the hotel last night? That he had spent the night at the farm...

Amber's lips curved in a faint smile. 'Yes, I know. Rory came to tell me last night. You'd better come in.'

Zoe looked incongruous standing there against a background of dark stone farm buildings, tall trees and drifting mist. Too fragile by far for this sombre Northern landscape in her fine pale grey suit with the rowan red silk blouse and matching high heeled red court shoes and clutch bag. Too smart. Too sophisticated. A stranger in a foreign land. A tropical bird of paradise in an alien country, and poor Laurie had thought that she would settle here and be content to become a farmer's wife!

As she entered the farm kitchen Zoe brought

with her a drift of some exotic perfume that Amber knew to be expensive. They faced one another across the big pine table, eyes wary, mouths set, each waiting for the other to speak. As she waited, Amber heard the soft sound of the fuel settling in the stove, the heavy ticking of the wall clock, the purring of the house cat.

'I've just come from the hospital,' Zoe said at last.

Amber clenched her hands and waited for her sister-in-law to go on.

'Laurie seemed pleased to see me.'

This was said too brightly, as though they were talking about some mutual friend. Amber winced, and searched her mind for words with which to reply.

'That's why I wanted you to come. Because he asked where you were as soon as he came out of the coma. He expected you to be with him. I don't think he could remember that you had left him.'

'I can't stay long because I have a lot of bookings for the next few weeks. Modelling and promotion work in London,' Zoe told her.

'Surely you won't want to upset Laurie by leaving again so soon? He might have a relapse,' Amber protested.

Zoe's lips tightened. 'I don't think you quite understand my position, Amber. My work is the most important thing in my life now.'

'More important than Laurie's recovery, you mean?'

Zoe shrugged her shoulders elegantly. 'Of course I'd like Laurie to get better, but I don't intend to sacrifice my career for him now that we are separated. You can't expect me to do that.'

The cold dislike for this girl which had been simmering inside Amber was now reaching boiling point and was ready to spill over.

'Don't you think you owe Laurie something, Zoe,' she snapped.

'What do you mean? I don't understand what you are trying to say. How could I owe anything to Laurie? I did my best to settle here. It was not my fault that I found life on this farm so intolerable that I had to get away from it.'

Anger erupted inside Amber then and found release in furious words that she hurled at her brother's wife without stopping to think whether or not they were justified.

'It's your fault that Laurie is lying where he is now! Your fault that he was so unhappy that he stopped taking proper care of himself and took the tractor where he knew it was dangerous to go. Tom said he had become very careless about his safety, after you went.'

'Tom is only a boy. He doesn't know what he's talking about. I'm surprised you take any notice of what he says,' Zoe said derisively.

'He's had to grow up fast since Laurie was injured, and work too hard for someone his age. I find it hard to forgive you for that,' Amber hit back.

'I still don't see how you can blame me for that,' Zoe protested.

'That's because you don't want to see, Zoe. You won't face up to what you did to us, to Laurie and me, when you started your affair with Rory.'

Zoe laughed. 'So that's what is at the bottom of all these accusations! Why you insist on blaming me. Because Rory was bored with you and preferred me! You can't blame me for that. If you spent a bit more time on making the best of your appearance Rory might not have fallen for me.'

'If you'd been a bit more loyal to Laurie, if you hadn't set out to get Rory right from the start, Laurie wouldn't have been where he is now. You've no right to shift the blame on to me, and you've no right to put your promotion work before staying here to help Laurie get better. He is your husband, after all. You are still married to him, aren't you?'

Zoe did not answer that at once but went to stare out of the window which gave a long view of the road to the village, and in the distance the gabled roof of the Edengate Hotel.

'I wouldn't have come at all, if Rory hadn't begged me to,' she said slowly. 'That's how much your brother means to me now.'

Amber took a deep breath, and fought against the despair that threatened to engulf her. Perhaps, after all, she had been wrong to go to so much trouble to bring Zoe back.

101

Maybe it would have been better to let Laurie remember, in his own good time, when and how his wife had left him. She felt sick and bewildered by the way things were going.

'What's the use of pretending?' Zoe went on. 'I made a mistake when I agreed to marry Laurie and come to live here. I hadn't known him for long enough, and I had no idea what it was going to be like living here with only the animals for company most of the time. I was very unhappy and bored, so I decided to cut my losses and leave. If you are harbouring any hopes of me staying on and going back to Laurie if he gets better you can forget them. I'll be going back to London quite soon. Unless,' she added with a sly little smile, 'Rory talks me into staying on with him in the hotel.'

'He won't,' Amber broke in. 'Because he told me last night that he's sorry for the way he treated me and that he wants me back.'

Zoe's smile deepened as she fired her final shot. Her victory salvo. 'Of course he'd have to say that, once you had allowed him to stay the night with you. You must be rather naive though if you believe him.'

With that she swung about and moved gracefully to the door that led into the yard. Then, without a backward glance, she stepped unhurriedly into Rory's car and set it in motion to take her back to Rory's hotel.

Amber watched her go with bitterness in her heart.

102

CHAPTER SEVEN

The days that followed Zoe's return to Edenby were even more difficult for Amber to cope with than the ones which had gone before. For one thing it was hard to endure the times when she was forced to sit beside Laurie's bed while Zoe occupied the chair at the other side. Invariably, whoever had been there first was soon making an excuse for leaving.

It was even harder having to listen to Laurie talk in that new, strange, careful way about what would happen when he went home to the farm, knowing as she did that Zoe would not be there to help him come to terms with the fact that his recovery was going to be a long, slow, and painful business.

Laurie had assumed that his wife was living at Edengate Farm with his twin sister and his younger brother, which meant that Amber and Tom were compelled to live a lie rather than let him learn the truth, because Sister Campbell had warned them that he was not yet strong enough to be reminded of the true state of his marriage. He had no memory, it seemed, of Zoe leaving him.

'It could set him back a lot to be reminded that his marriage had failed,' the sister maintained. 'After all, it's hard enough to come to terms with anything like that when you are well. In his state of health Mr Richards thinks he should be spared all stress for as long as possible. Of course, if he begins to get his memory back about the time before the accident it will be a different matter.'

'I don't know how to answer his questions, at times when he asks what Zoe is doing at the farm because she isn't visiting him. He just takes it for granted that she is helping with the work,' Amber said despairingly.

'Is she still staying at the Edengate Hotel?' the sister asked.

'Yes, she's still there.'

It had been necessary to give Zoe's address to the hospital as Laurie's next of kin.

The sister gave her a sympathetic glance. 'I know how hard it must be for you to behave as if you are on good terms with your sister-in-law, but really it is best to do so, for your brother's sake.'

Amber sighed. 'Yes, I know,' she murmured.

She had to make a great effort to keep her mind off all that Zoe's continued presence at the Edengate Hotel implied. How could she believe that Rory was telling the truth when he said he still cared for her, while Zoe was staying in his home, sharing meals with him, going riding with him sometimes? Amber would not let herself dwell on what else they might be doing together.

To Rory it was all quite simple and straightforward; Zoe would not stay at the farm with Amber and Tom, yet it was vital that she remained close at hand and visited Laurie regularly if he was to continue to recover from his terrible injuries. So what else could he do but allow her to stay on at the Edengate Hotel for the time being, and hope that Amber would understand that he was trying in this way to help Laurie?

As far as Amber was concerned it was not that simple, because Zoe had already stayed longer in Edenby than she had at first said she would, after making a short trip to London to fulfil a modelling contract. Amber had been forced then to tell Laurie that his wife had a heavy cold and had been forced to stay in bed. That set him worrying about her, and made Amber react angrily when Rory called at the farm one morning when she was alone there to ask her to go out for a meal with him.

'What would be the point in me going out for a meal with you, Rory, when there's no future for us now? It would be a waste of your time and mine, and I just don't have any time to waste now. There's always so much to do here, and the hospital visiting takes up so much of my time.'

'No wonder you look so tired and careworn,' he said in a voice that was so gentle that at first she felt herself soften towards him.

Then, as the true meaning of his words hit her, she winced. He was sorry for her because she was having a bad time, and because she

105

looked as if she was having a bad time. She knew that her hair was straggly and out of condition and that the jersey she wore for her jobs about the farm was faded and unflattering.

'Don't patronize me, Rory,' she snapped. 'I know how I look, and I know what a contrast I must make to Zoe, so why waste time on me when she's available on your own doorstep?'

'You know why, and it's nothing to do with feeling sorry for you or patronizing you, as you put it. If you come out for a meal with me it will give me the chance to convince you that I do still care about you.'

'How can you expect me to believe that? How can you expect me ever to trust you again?' she whispered.

'I thought, I hoped, that after I had got Zoe to come back here you might realize that I was trying to make amends for what happened.'

'I was grateful to you for that, and I am grateful to you for the help you've given me with the farm books. I don't know how I'd have managed without that and the help Fergus has given me with the fence repairing and some of the other jobs that were too heavy for Tom and me. We certainly couldn't have afforded to pay anyone to do all the work you and Fergus did.'

Rory frowned. 'Fergus seems to spend quite a bit of his spare time here,' he began. 'Maybe that's why—'

'Why shouldn't he?' she broke in. 'He's a good friend to me and to Tom.'

'Especially to you, I suppose?' This last was said with a trace of a sneer.

'Yes.'

Until that moment when she heard the sneer in Rory's voice she had not stopped to think, because of her frantic, work-filled days, just how much she had come to value her friendship with Fergus. How much she had come to like him and depend on him for help and advice. Fergus was someone on whom she could rely not just for help but for understanding of her problems. She thought of the way Fergus had managed to talk Tom out of his constant wish to absent himself from school to work on the farm. The way he would spend his free time doing some of the heaviest and dirtiest jobs about the farm so that she would no longer have to worry about getting them done. The way he made her laugh with his stories of his animal patients and their owners. Fergus was someone who offered her uncomplicated friendship and trust. Someone whose presence in her life aroused no doubts or fears, no jealousies or heartaches. Fergus was becoming very important to her.

'Is Fergus Carew the reason why you won't come out with me?' Rory asked when she had remained silent for too long.

All at once then she knew that he had offered her an escape route. A means of severing, once and for all, the strong bond of physical attraction which Rory knew still existed between him and her even though her faith in him had been destroyed by his affair with Zoe.

'Yes, Rory, I suppose he is,' she said very slowly so that the words should sink into his consciousness as well as her own. 'I really do like Fergus rather a lot.'

Rory's lips tightened. 'I suppose I've only myself to blame for that,' he said bitterly.

She did not answer. Did not meet his eyes but kept her own downcast on the house cat who was rubbing round her ankles.

'Yet there is still something between us, Amber. I know there is. If I were to take you in my arms right now you wouldn't be able to deny it, however much you may think you like Fergus Carew.'

He took a step towards her, as though he intended to prove what he had just said to her. A wild surge of panic invaded her mind as she tensed her body ready to resist him if he came any nearer. Then her heart gave a great lurch of relief as she heard the dogs begin to bark out in the yard as a vehicle came to a halt there. She craned her neck to look out of the window, and laughed shakily as she recognized the vehicle.

'Talking of Fergus, here he is now!'

'Just in time, I'd say. But there will be other times, Amber, my darling. I haven't given up yet, and I don't intend to. So you'd better remember that.' Rory smiled as he said the words, but his eyes were serious.

Amber moved towards the door that led into the yard, intent on greeting Fergus. Rory also moved that way, so that he and Fergus met on the doorstep.

'I've just come from the hotel,' the vet told the hotel owner. 'I thought I'd just take another look at Kelly to make sure his leg was healing properly while I was over this way.'

'And is it?' Rory's face was unsmiling.

'Yes, it's clearing up quite well. You'll be able to ride him again in a couple of days, if you take it easy at first.'

'Good! Thanks, Fergus.' Then, after a moment of hesitation, Rory went on: 'Are you here to visit a patient too, or is it just a social call today?'

Fergus grinned. 'Just a social call. Taking advantage of the chance to see Amber while I'm passing the farm on my way from your place. I'll be seeing you next week if you are going to the Animal Rescue Centre supper dance at Middleby. Your father just bought a couple of tickets from me because he thought you might like to go.'

'Then I'll be there, and maybe Amber as well?' Rory threw a questioning glance at her.

She looked away from the glance and ignored his words.

'Yes, Amber will be there. That's one of the reasons I called in, to arrange what time I'll be picking her up,' Fergus was saying.

Amber moved her startled gaze from Rory to Fergus, then back again to Rory.

He gave her a rueful smile. 'That means I'll probably ask Zoe to go with me, if she's still here.'

'She doesn't seem to be in any hurry to leave you, does she? Or to move up here with Amber and Tom.' A challenging stare accompanied these words from Fergus and brought a faint smile from Amber.

'No. Things are becoming rather difficult,' Rory said slowly. 'I'm beginning to wish I'd never suggested she should stay at the hotel.'

'It's very difficult for us all,' Amber broke in. 'All this pretence about where Zoe is staying. All this deceit! I'll glad when there is no need for it any more. When Laurie is strong enough to be told the truth about Zoe.'

'Won't we all?' Rory snapped as he strode away towards his car.

Fergus grinned at Amber as they listened together to the sound of his car speeding away down the hill.

'It seems the glamorous Zoe is causing problems for Rory, even becoming a liability to him,' Fergus remarked as he moved further into the kitchen and closer to Amber.

'As she is to us all! Oh Fergus, I wonder how it will all end? Will Laurie suddenly remember one day that she walked out on him? If he does, what will that do to him?'

Fergus put a comforting hand on her

shoulder. 'What do they say at the hospital? Do they think there is any likelihood of him remembering?'

Her troubled frown deepened. 'Sister Campbell says you can never really be sure what will happen in cases like his. The specialist won't commit himself either, so we'll just have to wait and see, and hope for the best. But it does put such a strain on Tom and me having to behave as if Zoe is spending most of her time here with us when she's not at the hospital, when we've no idea what she is doing.' She paused, then added, 'Or who she is with.'

'Is there any chance at all that she'll go back to him when he is fit again?' Fergus asked, stroking her shoulder gently so that she felt the tension gradually easing away.

'I don't think so. Certainly not if Laurie is fit enough to go back to farming. She said she hated the life here and found it so boring that she just couldn't put up with it any longer. In fact when she came back to see Laurie she told me that her career came first with her now and that she wouldn't give it up for anyone. I'm really surprised that she has stayed so long. I keep expecting her to go back to London, or not to come back when she goes to do these days of modelling or promotions work there. I don't know what I'd say to Laurie then. I feel so frightened sometimes, Fergus, about what is going to happen to Laurie, and to Tom and me.'

Fergus took both of her hands in his own strong, square hands and held them tightly, as though trying to convey some of his own strength and courage to her. His lips brushed her tousled hair and she knew that it did not matter to him that she was untidy and not looking her best. Fergus would love her as much on her bad days as on her good ones, the thought came to her then. Her eyes stung with the effort of keeping tears at bay as he drew her into his arms.

'Poor darling, you've had such a rotten time! Nothing but too much hard work and worry, with no time for fun and relaxation to help you cope. We really must do something about that. We'll start with the Animal Rescue Centre dance, and go on from there. I know this is probably the wrong time to tell you, Amber my love, but I'm serious about you. Very serious. I want you to remember that and to tell yourself when you are feeling low that I'm here waiting to give you some happier times.'

Amber blinked away the tears. 'Oh, Fergus, you are such a special person! I've never known anyone quite like you before.'

His kiss was long, but tender and restrained. 'And I knew from the first time I met you that you were going to be important to me.'

Her eyes searched his face as she allowed herself to relax against his sturdy body.

'Do you mean when we met at the scene of

the accident that day, when Chance wouldn't allow you to come too near me?'

'No, I mean when we met for the first time, at the Moorcock Inn, after you ran into Lucky.'

She was bewildered by that. 'How could you know then, when we only spent those few moments together and I was in such a miserable mood?'

He chuckled. 'I just knew! I couldn't forget about you, you see. I was always looking out for you when I came over this way and I couldn't understand why you were never anywhere to be seen. I even called here one day and made the excuse that I'd been given a wrong address for a visit from my receptionist. That was the first time I met your sister-in-law, but I wasn't interested in her. It was you I wanted to find.'

Now it was her turn to smile. 'You'd have had to come to Scotland to find me, Fergus,' she explained. 'I got the job up in the Highlands very soon after we met at the Moorcock.'

His face was more serious now. 'I found myself worrying about you as well as wondering because of how upset you were at the pub that day when I came to treat the injured puppy. I was convinced it was not just because of the puppy being injured that you were so upset. After all, Lucky wasn't very badly hurt, was he?'

Amber hesitated. She had known from the

113

odd remark he had made on a previous occasion that he was curious about that day, but he had never asked her about it openly. He might be aware, because of local gossip gathered as he went about his work in the area, that she had been engaged to Rory once, just as he was also likely to have heard that Rory and Zoe had been having an affair, but he could not know the truth about that day because Amber had spoken of it to no-one except Rory and Zoe. It had been locked away inside her ever since, giving her pain like a raw nerve touched, whenever she thought of it. Perhaps now was the time to share that hurt with someone? Someone who would understand and sympathize, as Fergus surely would. He was waiting now for her to speak.

She sighed, and began her explanation. 'No, it was not just the shock of running into the puppy that upset me so much, Fergus. It was what happened while I was waiting for you to arrive. You see I saw Rory there, with Zoe, who was supposed to be visiting an invalid aunt who was in a nursing home. They were sitting very close together, so close that you didn't need much imagination to see how things were between them. It was all there in their body language, and it was such a shock to me because I had no idea that Zoe had been unfaithful to Laurie, or that Rory had been deceiving me,' she added in a barely audible whisper.

Fergus remained silent, knowing that she needed time to go on and unburden herself of all the bitterness and pain she had endured on that day and afterwards. He began to stroke her hair.

'I was so shocked at first that I just stood there and watched them, and they were so absorbed with one another that they did not see me. I couldn't believe it was happening, until I saw them touching, and kissing. I felt as if I couldn't move, and I kept remembering little things like the way I sometimes called in at the farm if I was going shopping for the Country Club kitchen and found Rory there talking to Zoe while Laurie was away at the auction mart or looking at the sheep. Or the way Rory was so often making excuses about not being able to go with me to look for furniture for the flat we were supposed to be furnishing at the hotel for when we were married. I had wanted him to go shopping with me that day, but he had said he was too busy. Oh Fergus, I felt so let down, so humiliated, so rejected that I wanted to die. Then the puppy wriggled out of my arms and ran across the room barking, and Rory looked up and saw me.'

'What did he say?' Fergus asked quietly.

'They both pretended that it was an accidental meeting, but they had guilt written all over them. Then you arrived and I went into the garden so you could examine the puppy.

115

You were very kind to me, Fergus. You brought me some coffee and told me not to be upset, that the puppy was not much hurt.'

'And all the time it was you being hurt. What did you do about it? Did you tell your brother what you had discovered?'

She shook her head. 'No. I never told him anything about it. Zoe was waiting for me when I arrived back and she tried to convince me that they never planned the meeting, that they had simply run into one another by chance. I knew she was not telling the truth, but she said Laurie would never believe me if I tried to tell him what I had seen. I knew she was right, because he worshipped her and would take her word as against mine. So I said nothing.'

'What about Rory? What did he have to say about it?'

'He said it was partly my own fault, for postponing our wedding when my mother was very ill. So I gave him back his ring, and went to Scotland.'

'He was a fool to let you go.'

'No, Fergus, I was the fool for not seeing what was going on right under my nose between him and Zoe. The way she was always so keen to visit a poor old dear who often didn't even know she was there. The way Rory was so often at the farm when Laurie was away from it. I thought it was just coincidence, until I found them together at the Moorcock.' She

116

stopped, and bit her lip, then said 'You must think me very naive, Fergus?'

Fergus lifted her chin with his finger and kissed her lips lightly, teasingly. 'No more so than I was when I went chasing after the wrong woman just because I thought if I persisted she was bound to fall for me one day. I couldn't see that she'd already fallen for someone else.' He laughed softly. 'But our mistakes are in the past now and we have a chance to make a new beginning, if we take it, Amber.'

It was such a wonderful prospect, that of linking her future with that of this kind, funny, sensitive man, yet even as her spirits lifted at the thought the shadow of Laurie's accident intruded. How could she even consider making a new life for herself when Laurie needed her so much? She moved away from Fergus, gently but quite firmly.

'What's the use of making plans, the way things are for me now?' she said bleakly.

'Things won't always be the way they are now. Think of a future which includes trips to the theatre, dinner-dances, picnics, fell walking, and of course night calls that have to be answered and bills that have to be sent out time and time again before the money comes in,' Fergus told her with a smile.

Amber found her cheeks burning. 'Oh, Fergus, I hope we don't owe you any money! I'm so behind with the bookkeeping—'

Fergus laughed. 'I've no idea, but just in

case, I'll collect a little on account.'

He moved swiftly to take her in his arms and this time his kiss was so warm and passionate that her heart began to race. She was sorry when he drew away from her and said he must be going or he'd be late for his surgery in Middleby.

When he had gone there still seemed to be a lightness in the atmosphere, a lingering warmth and joy that had been brought to her by his presence. As she went back to her tasks about the farmhouse Amber felt comforted by the ray of hope he had brought to her future.

Laurie's slow but definite improvement continued in the days that followed, though there was still some doubt about how fully he would recover. Zoe's visits also continued, but according to Sister Campbell were becoming briefer and less frequent.

'I suppose one can't blame her. It must be rather awful for her to have to sit there pretending that all is well between her and Laurie when she knows it isn't,' the young nursing sister said thoughtfully.

'I'm surprised that she's still here. She said when she first came that she wouldn't be staying long because of her career commitments.' Yet even as Amber said that she knew why Zoe was staying on. It was simply so that she could be near to Rory. A shiver of fear ran down her back as she wondered what would happen when Laurie was well enough to be allowed home.

'Mr Richards says your brother may be able to come home in a couple of weeks if he continues to make good progress,' Sister Campbell told her then. 'He'll have to come back for physiotherapy a couple of times a week but it will make life easier for you, won't it? Visiting here every evening at the end of a long day's work can be very tiring.'

'I don't mind, so long as Laurie is getting better. I'll have to come a bit earlier tomorrow evening because I'm going to a dinner-dance.'

Sister Campbell smiled. 'That's just what you need now. Something to give you a change from all the hard work and worry you've had. I hope you have a happy time.'

Just for that evening she would put aside all her worries about the future, Amber decided as she got ready for the dance after her early visit to the hospital. Tom had stayed at home to cope with the milking, helped by Fergus who was off duty. Now Fergus had gone back to his cottage to shower and change before coming to collect her.

'How do I look?' she asked Tom when she went downstairs in the midnight blue dress which fitted her slender figure to perfection and left her smooth shoulders bare.

Tom whistled his appreciation. 'Brilliant! You ought to get dressed up more often, Ambie.'

Amber laughed at that. 'What, for milking

119

and foddering up and collecting the eggs?'

'She used to. Zoe, I mean.'

'But she didn't get involved with the work much, did she?'

'No. She did it so she could get involved with your guy, Rory,' Tom said with the brutal frankness of his youth.

'He's not my guy now, Tom,' she told him. 'He's just a friend who comes here to help us sometimes.'

'He won't be able to do that when Laurie comes home, will he?'

'Why not?' she asked, with uneasiness beginning to stir inside her.

'Because Laurie is starting to remember what happened before the accident.'

Her eyes widened with astonishment. 'What makes you think that, Tom?'

'Something he said.'

'When?'

'Yesterday, while you were away from his bed talking to that nice sister from Scotland.'

Amber felt her throat swell with emotion. 'What did he say, Tom?' she whispered. 'What did he say?'

CHAPTER EIGHT

Amber stared at her young brother, hardly able to believe what he had told her, and at the 'ergus,' she agreed.

...t of the evening she succeeded, with ...n doing just that as the superb meal ...ed in the dining room of an ancient ...urious coaching inn. The dancing ...ame later beneath disco lights in a ...ted coach house behind the main hotel ...g was equally enjoyable because despite ...urdy body Fergus turned out to be very ...on his feet and to possess a good sense of ...thm. It was sheer pleasure to move with him ...ough dance after dance, until it was time for ...n to do his duty and invite his senior ...rtner's middle-aged wife to dance.

It was then that Rory appeared at Amber's ...ide. She had seen him earlier, dining at a nearby table and dancing with Zoe and several other partners, but she had not expected him to get to her so swiftly the moment Fergus had gone.

'Hello, Amber! My dance, I think.'

Without waiting for her to answer he steered her on to the floor and held her closely. Too closely for her comfort or peace of mind, so that she tensed her body and tried to pull herself away from him.

'Don't!' she said fiercely.

'Don't what?' he teased, holding her tighter still so that she felt almost welded to him.

'Don't hold me so tightly! People are staring at us.'

'Why shouldn't they? We make a handsome

124

same time wondering why he had not mentioned it earlier; why nothing had been said about it at the hospital that afternoon. Of course she usually got her progress reports from Sister Campbell, who had cared for Laurie since the day of his accident, but there had been an emergency admission during her brief visit which had claimed the attention of all the medical staff.

'What did Laurie say, Tom?' she asked again.

'It was when you went to see Sister Campbell, while Laurie was asleep—'

'Yes! Go on! Hurry, or Fergus will be here for me.'

'Just as Laurie began to wake up he said "Zoe" and began to look around as though he thought she might be there. Then he muttered to himself something like "No, she wouldn't be here. She went away a long time ago. Left me, didn't she?"'

Amber held her breath and waited for Tom to go on.

'He closed his eyes then and went to sleep again, and I sat there wondering what to do if he woke again and asked me about Zoe. Then you came back and said it was time for us to leave.'

'Did he seem to be upset, when he talked about Zoe going away?'

Tom shook his head. 'Not really. More sort of surprised, as if he'd forgotten about her

121

leaving him and only just remembered about it then.'

Amber frowned. 'Maybe he didn't mean it like that. Perhaps he just meant that Zoe had left after her latest visit?'

Tom did not agree with that. 'I don't think so, somehow.'

'Yet he didn't mention it to me when I went to see him this afternoon. In fact he didn't say much at all. Why didn't you mention it before, Tom?'

He laughed. 'Well, if you remember, I fell asleep in the car going home and you made me go straight up to bed when we got home because I was too tired to do my homework. Then this morning I slept in and had to eat my breakfast on the school bus, so there was no time for talking.' His face sobered then. 'What will you do about it, Ambie?' he worried.

'I don't know, Tom. I just don't know. Perhaps I'll ask Sister Campbell's advice.'

Their troubled glances met across the room for a long moment before a great commotion broke out in the yard as Chance and Risky signalled the arrival of Fergus.

'We'll talk about it tomorrow,' she promised. 'Don't wait up for me tonight, I'll probably be very late.'

'I won't! Have a good time, Ambie.'

'I will!' she called over her shoulder as she slid into her white wool jacket and went to join Fergus in the frosty, starlit yard.

122

'I've been looking fo[rward to] Fergus told her as [they] village and heade[d for] market town where [the func]tion

'So have I,' she ad[mitted.]

She gave him a smile [along] and he touched her hand [briefly] the car down where th[e] narrowed.

'How was Laurie today?' [he] later as they sped along the alm[ost]

'He's still improving. He is to b[e] a general ward tomorrow and he mi[ght] able to come home in a couple of w[eeks.]

'Then you'll have some explaining won't you? About his wife, I mean.'

'Yes.'

She wondered whether to tell him what [Tom] had said about Laurie's memory beginning come back, but was there really anything to tell? Could Tom have been mistaken in what he thought he had heard their brother say when he was still half asleep?

'It might be a good idea to prepare him before he comes home,' Fergus suggested into her silence. 'It may not come as such a shock to him then.'

'I'll have to think about that,' she murmured.

'But not tonight, darling,' he said firmly. 'Tonight is for forgetting all of your problems and just being happy. Right?'

123

couple, don't you think?'

'Not any more! We are not a couple any more. That ended when you took up with Zoe. You know it did.'

'Not as far as I'm concerned. I told you on the night I stayed at the farm to do the VAT returns for you that I still wanted you.'

'That wasn't what Zoe said when she came to the farm the next day. She said—' Amber broke off then; she could not go on to tell him that her sister-in-law thought Rory had spent the night in her bed rather than asleep in a chair over the books, and that she had tried to convince Amber that Rory's declaration that he still cared for her had been made only so that she would allow him to stay and make love to her.

Rory's fingers dug into her back. 'Go on, Amber,' he urged. 'Tell me just what Zoe said.'

Now she found the courage to do that, because she had to know whether what Zoe had told her was true.

'She said you had just been using me, and telling me you still cared about me to justify it, so that I'd let you stay the night. She said it was her you still wanted.'

'And you believed her?'

'Why shouldn't I? All the evidence was on her side, you'd had an affair with her and she was still staying in your home.'

'My hotel,' he corrected her.

'She's still staying there, in spite of the fact

125

that she was only supposed to be there for a few days.'

'Damn it, Amber! I told you—' His voice was rising, and so was her embarrassment. 'You've got to believe me. I knew as soon as I saw you again that I had been a fool to risk losing you. We've got to talk about this; to get things sorted out.'

'There's nothing to sort out, Rory. You've been a good friend to help me with the books, but that's all you are to me now. Just a friend. We can't go back to the way things were.'

'We can! We will, if you'll just give me a chance. I'll tell Zoe she must find somewhere else to stay.'

'It won't make any difference, and she'll be going soon anyway.'

'What do you mean?'

'I mean that Laurie is beginning to remember that she left him, so there will be no need to go on with the pretence.'

'I wondered how long it would be before he remembered what had happened. She won't go back to him you know.'

'I don't want her to go back to him,' Amber interrupted. 'Laurie deserves somebody better than her. She's selfish, and deceitful, and not to be trusted.'

Rory interrupted this time. 'Zoe's not all bad, you know. She's just someone who is used to having what she wants from life. She thought she wanted your brother, but she

126

couldn't cope with his way of life and she found it boring and frustrating living on a farm.'

'Until she found you to amuse herself with, and to defend her bad behaviour!' Amber hit back.

'Only so that you might try to understand and to give me another chance, Amber darling.' As he spoke, Rory was trying to urge her away from the dancers and through an archway on to a glassed in balcony that overlooked the river, a place furnished with cane chairs and sofas. A place much more private than the disco room. Panic began to rise in her, then a surge of relief enveloped her as she spotted Zoe following them through the arch into the conservatory.

'Zoe is looking for you, and I must get back to Fergus,' she said breathlessly, beginning to pull out of his grasp.

'Wait—' Rory begged.

'There's no point. I've nothing more to say to you,' she managed in the moment before Zoe reached them.

With her mind in a turmoil, she did not after all go back to Fergus at once but instead made for the powder room. After splashing her face and hands with cool water she seated herself before one of the elegant little dressing tables and began to comb out her hair, then to apply powder to her nose. She was alone in the room, and glad of it. Then, just as she decided she was calm enough to return to the disco room, the door opened and Zoe came in to stand behind her. Amber did not turn round but stared at her sister-in-law's reflection in the mirror and waited for her to speak.

'You still think you'll get Rory back, don't you?' Zoe said, with a triumphant glitter in the green eyes that were an exact match for her low-cut dress.

'I could have him, if I wanted. He just said so,' Amber heard herself reply.

Zoe laughed. 'And of course you believed him! How naive you are still, Amber. Rory knows I'll never give up my career for any man, and he knows just as well that you, with your catering college diploma and your liking for the country lifestyle, would make an ideal wife for a country hotel owner. Especially one whose father says it's time he settled down and brought a wife in as a working partner.'

Amber forced a laugh. 'You are making it up Zoe! Henry would never put that sort of pressure on Rory.'

'He would if he was forced to take his doctor's advice seriously.'

'What do you mean? Henry isn't ill, is he?' Concern for Henry Ashton, of whom she had always been fond, banished all else from Amber's mind.

'He is certainly not well. The doctor has been to the hotel twice in the last few days and done cardiograph tests on him. Henry has been warned to take life easily now, and to consider

128

retirement very seriously.'

Amber's concern deepened. 'Rory didn't say anything about it to me.'

'Perhaps he wanted to make certain he got you back, first,' Zoe said mockingly.

Amber did not know what to believe, she would question Rory about his father later. For now she changed the subject to one she was equally worried about.

'How much longer are you planning on staying, Zoe?' she asked bluntly. 'I'd like to know, for Laurie's sake.'

'I'm leaving tomorrow. The doctor says Laurie is strong enough to be told the truth, so I shall tell him tomorrow morning then leave for London because I have a lot of work lined up there and in Italy. Don't ask me to go back to him, Amber. You would be wasting your time and mine.'

Amber rose to her feet to give her answer. 'I wasn't going to, because I know you would never make Laurie happy. You are too selfish to do that.'

She did not stay to hear Zoe's answer but left the powder room at once and went in search of Fergus.

'I wondered where you had got to,' Fergus greeted her. 'I saw you dancing with Rory, then you simply seemed to disappear.' There was a question in his eyes that told her he was not yet sure of her.

'I went to the powder room to get rid of my

shiny nose,' she told him with a smile.

'Would you like another glass of wine? Or to dance again?' he asked then as the air began to throb again with the beat of a new disco dance.

Suddenly then Amber knew that what she wanted most was to be away from the wine and the music and the dancing. Away from the heat and the noise and the people. Away from any more meetings with either Rory or Zoe. 'What I'd really like is to go home now, Fergus,' she admitted. 'To drive home nice and slowly with the windows right down and lots of fresh air coming into the car.'

His face became anxious. 'You are not feeling ill, or upset?'

Amber laughed softly. 'Oh no! Just rather tired. I seem to have got out of the habit of staying up this late. Or this early in the morning,' she added after a glance at her watch.

Fergus chuckled. 'Yes, I know what you mean. It's ages since I went to this sort of affair, and I was thinking while I was waiting for you to come back that there was too much noise and not enough fresh air for me. Let's go now!'

'I'll get my coat.'

With luck they would be away before Rory could join them, she thought as she saw him threading his way in their direction, but he was too quick for her.

'You are not leaving already, are you?' he challenged them. 'There's still an hour of dancing to go.'

'Not for us,' Fergus told him. 'Amber feels like some fresh air, so we are going to enjoy a nice leisurely drive home over the moors.'

Rory was not pleased to hear that. 'I was going to ask you to dance again,' he said to Amber.

'I've had all the dancing I want, for tonight,' she responded. Then 'You didn't tell me that Henry was ill, did you?'

He flushed. 'I would have done, if you'd stayed with me a bit longer. I suppose Zoe has been talking to you?'

'Yes. She put me in the picture about how things are with Henry, and what he wants you to do.'

'I'd have told you that, too, if you had given me the chance. You know I would.'

His eyes pleaded with her to believe him, but she was a different person now from the girl who had fallen in love with him when she was still only a schoolgirl, and believed everything he told her. The events of the last year had shown her the flaws in Rory's character and convinced her that she would never be able to trust him fully again, and what was love without trust? Had it ever been love, anyway, or merely a strong physical attraction between her and Rory? The physical attraction was still there, she knew, but she was also mature enough to know she needed more than that from the man she chose to share her life with.

She needed what Fergus could give her.

'I hope Henry will soon be better. Give him my regards,' she said as Fergus brought her soft white wool jacket and slipped it about her shoulders before slipping an arm through hers, and with a brief 'goodnight' to Rory Fergus led her outside to where his car was parked.

It was good to feel the sharp, frosty air biting into her face and to feel the trembling inside her subsiding now that she had left Rory behind. There had been a surge of emotion filling her as she walked away with Fergus; a deep thankfulness that at last she had been able to see Rory as he really was. Now she knew that she had made the right decision and was free to love someone else. Free to love Fergus.

The moors stretched, moonlit and empty of all except hundreds of grazing sheep, as Fergus drove at a leisurely speed away from Middleby and in the direction of Edenby. He did not speak to her while he was driving, as though he sensed her need to have a breathing space in which to come to terms with the decision she had just made. Soon Amber was relaxing in her seat, and content that it should be Fergus in the one next to her, his burly left shoulder clad in the unfamiliar garb of dinner jacket and stark white shirt touching her own right one so that she could feel the warmth of him through the thin white jacket she wore.

All at once then she found herself feeling happy in a way she had not experienced for a very long time. There was a rightness about sitting beside Fergus at the end of an enjoyable evening, about knowing that Fergus would become more and more a part of her life, and that she would become part of his. Part of his home and his work, maybe. There seemed to be a rightness about that too.

From time to time as the miles rolled slowly away from them the ghostly grey shapes of sheep would loom ahead on the narrow winding road and Fergus would patiently wait for them to wander away again.

After one such wait he did not gather speed again but instead steered his car into a parking place beside the stream that meandered over the moor. He switched off the engine, and let his hands lie idle on the steering wheel. There was no sound to be heard then except for the soft murmur of the water as it ran beneath a hump-backed bridge. She turned to Fergus, smiling, waiting.

Fergus was staring straight ahead of him, his gaze searching the peaceful moonlit landscape while he cast about in his mind for words to say to her. Yet his silence was not oppressive, rather it was comforting because she knew that what he had to say was important and the words he chose would not be lightly uttered. At last he was ready, and he turned to her then with compassion in his eyes.

'Is Rory Ashton pestering you to go back to him, Amber?' he asked very quietly. 'I saw him seek you out a couple of times this evening and I wondered. Especially as I knew Zoe was leaving soon.'

'Did you think he only wanted me back because she was going? Or that he would have wanted me back anyway?'

'Did that matter to you, Amber? Why he wants you back, I mean. You haven't denied that he does—'

'No. Does it matter so much to you, Fergus, how I feel about Rory now?' she murmured.

'Of course it does! I don't want to see you hurt again, as you would be hurt by him sooner or later. And I don't want to be hurt myself,' he added, less vehemently.

'Oh Fergus, I won't be hurt by Rory ever again because I won't ever feel about him again as I once did. I'm cured of that. I could never trust him, never believe him as I once did.'

'When I saw him holding you so tightly I was mad with jealousy. I wondered if you were enjoying it, as I knew he was.'

'I was more worried about the embarrassment of being seen like that with him, after everyone knew about him and Zoe. I can't rid myself of the feeling that he is still attracted to Zoe, in spite of what he says. I could never share the man in my life, Fergus. I want more commitment from the man I love than that,' she told him.

Fergus smiled as he put his hands on her shoulders and drew her close. 'You'll have more commitment from me, Amber, I can promise you. You'll have total commitment, always.'

She lifted her mouth to meet his and gave a long shiver of delight as the warmth and passion of his kisses invaded her senses. This was a new Fergus, she was discovering. Beneath the plain, square face and the quiet manner was a man who could stir her emotionally and physically as no one had ever done before.

Time ceased to exist for either of them as the moon shone down brilliantly and frost changed the dark heather covered moor to a dazzling whiteness. For tonight this beautiful place, this enchanted hour, belonged only to them and their love. It was only much later, as cars leaving Middleby at the end of the dinner-dance to drive to Edenby began to pass them in increasing numbers, that they became aware of how late it must be.

'I suppose I'll have to let you go, take you home, dearest?' Fergus said reluctantly. 'Though I don't want to. I want to keep you here, all to myself.' Amber moved in his arms, dazed with happiness and unwilling to emerge from that state. Then she remembered that Tom was alone in the farmhouse. What if there should be a phone call from the hospital, a new crisis for Laurie? How would he cope with it? She must get back to him.

'Yes, we must go. I have to get home

135

to Tom.'

Already she was sitting up straight in her seat, attempting to tidy her clothes and her hair, looking at Fergus with a sleepy radiance about her as she said 'But I don't want to leave you. You know that, don't you Fergus?'

'Yes, but it's good to hear you say it. I'd better take you home though,' he laughed. 'Or Tom will be waiting for me with a shotgun!'

They both chuckled at the picture this brought of the boy standing up to the tall, strongly built young vet, but Fergus set the car in motion and lost no more time in getting Amber to the gate of her home. It was there, as he gave her one last immeasurably long embrace at the entrance to the farm that a dark cloud threatened her new-found joy.

'I don't want to wait long to marry you darling,' Fergus whispered as he released her. 'Think about an Easter wedding. Easter is early this year.'

Amber was startled. 'Easter! Oh, Fergus, I can't marry you as soon as that.'

'Why not? You love me, and you've said you will marry me?'

'But Laurie will hardly have had time to get home again by then, and he won't be able to manage without me to help him. Nor will Tom.'

'You can't sacrifice your whole future for your brothers, Amber,' Fergus said stiffly. 'They can't expect you to do that. They can get

136

a housekeeper, surely. I've had to manage with a housekeeper since I came to the practice here.'

'There isn't the money available to pay for a housekeeper, Fergus. We are struggling as it is, just to keep the farm going,' she pointed out.

'Laurie wouldn't want you to give up your own chance of happiness for him, surely?'

'I wouldn't be giving it up, just postponing it until Laurie is well enough to be able to cope.'

'If he ever does,' Fergus said sombrely, facing a fact that Amber would not even consider.

'He will get better, eventually, and we could still be together Fergus as often as possible even if we didn't get married yet. You would know that I belonged to you—'

'I don't want that kind of togetherness for us! I want the old fashioned kind with marriage, a home of our own and a family when we want one, not when it fits in with other people's plans. Isn't that what you want?'

'Yes, of course, but there's still Laurie and Tom—'

His arms dropped from about her. 'Perhaps you don't love me enough to put my needs first?'

Her eyes began to sting with the hurt his words brought. She took a deep breath before she answered him.

'I know it's not fair to ask you to wait, Fergus, but I don't know what else I can do. I just don't know.'

Fergus looked down into her face, his own features set in stern lines as he uttered his final words to her.

'Think hard before you ruin both our lives, and Laurie's, because he won't thank you for making him feel a burden to you.'

Then he bent to kiss her again, but without passion, before opening the farm gate to let her through. When he closed the gate again after she had passed through it she watched him walk away, and felt a terrible sadness creep over her.

CHAPTER NINE

For most of that night Amber lay wide awake, tossing and turning in her bed as she went over the things she had said to Fergus, and the things Fergus had said to her. There was bitter sweetness in recalling the joy of belonging to Fergus for that brief enchanted time, but despair in having to acknowledge that there was no chance of their being able to marry and live together in the near future while Laurie and Tom still needed her so much.

Life had been cruel to her again, to send her Fergus to love at a time when she was not free to give all of her time to him. Fergus deserved better than that. It was not fair to expect him to enter into a long engagement with her; to ask him to wait for marriage as she had asked Rory to wait. It had ended in disaster with Rory, and it would surely do so with Fergus. So she must let him go, before he had time to become too important to her, and she to him.

Wasn't it already too late, though, for that? Because she had not committed herself to him lightly last night; she had not been carried away by the moonlight, the wine and the sight of Fergus looking so marvellous in his dinner jacket instead of his shabby working clothes. She had given herself to him because he seemed so right for her in a way no one had ever done before. Not even Rory. There was no regret in her for that, because Fergus was so worthy of her love. He had been a tower of strength to her in the dark days of despair she had lived through since coming back to Edengate and the thought of giving up his friendship brought hurt to her mind. The thought of giving up his love brought an unbearable agony.

What else could she do, though, when Laurie would be coming home from hospital in a couple of weeks with no wife to look after him? He would need someone with him for weeks, maybe months. Perhaps for ever. It was not duty that forced her to be that someone, it was love for her twin; her childhood playmate, her protector, her other half. If there was a price to be paid for looking after her twin and that price was the sacrifice of her own happiness, then she would have to accept it. The Wakefields of Edengate Farm had always been a close family and now, with both parents dead, they were closer than ever because they could not survive without one another.

When she could bear her soul searching no longer, Amber got up and made tea, taking up a mug for Tom. Getting him to wake up was not easy, he was showing the signs of strain and overtiredness more and more as the winter strengthened its grip on the rugged countryside and made the work of the farm even harder.

'Oh, I wish it was Saturday, or Sunday, and I didn't have to go to school!' he groaned.

'It'll be easier when Laurie comes home,' she tried to comfort him. 'It won't be long now.'

Later, when the milking was done and they were sharing a breakfast that Amber had no appetite for, she told Tom that Zoe was leaving Edenby that day and going back to London.

'She might as well, for all the good she's done here,' Tom grunted in the voice that was deepening rapidly as he neared his fifteenth birthday.

'Yes,' she agreed. 'But I'm dreading going to see Laurie today, because she's going to tell him this morning that she won't ever go back to him. She says his doctor thinks he is strong enough to be able to take the truth now.'

'I think he's remembered anyway,' Tom said with his mouth full of bacon and egg. 'I told you last night that he had.'

140

'We can't be certain, though, can we?'

'He'll be better off without her. He's got us, we'll look after him,' Tom answered as he reached for more toast.

Amber frowned. 'We know he'll be better off without her, but he doesn't. What if he has a relapse when he knows she's going for good? He's been doing so well lately, since he started having physiotherapy. He's been much more cheerful too.'

Tom stopped eating and looked at her with the new maturity which had come to him in recent weeks. 'Don't worry too much, Ambie. He has to know about Zoe. We couldn't go on pretending for ever that she was living here with us, not now he's nearly ready to come home.'

'No, but I'm still just dreading today. I think, if you don't mind, I'll go to see him late this afternoon instead of waiting until tonight. I want to be there as soon as I can after Zoe has left. Besides, the weather forecast is very bad for later in the day. They say it's going to snow, so I'll get there before it comes, I hope.'

'Shall I come to the hospital straight from school instead of coming home on the school bus?' Tom asked then.

She hesitated, then shook her head. 'No, I think you'd better come straight home in case the bad weather arrives early.'

Amber half expected him to protest at that but instead he looked relieved. He had

141

probably been dreading having to face Laurie today as much as she was, she thought.

'I'll come home on the bus and get on with the milking,' he agreed, then added 'Did you have a good time last night at the dance?'

'Yes, I did.'

'I never heard you come back. I suppose it was very late. Or very early!'

'Yes, very early. Fergus thought you might be waiting for him with a shotgun,' she told him.

He let out a shout of laughter. 'I like Fergus. He's a great guy, isn't he?'

'Yes,' she said again. 'He certainly is!' Then, since it hurt so much to talk about Fergus, she added, 'You'd better get a move on Tom or you'll miss the bus.'

She watched from the window as he dashed across the yard, calling a word of farewell to the two dogs, who knew better than to try to follow him when he was wearing school uniform and carrying a satchel. As she carried her untouched breakfast into the yard to give to the dogs she shivered and looked about her at the darkening landscape. To the east, beyond the fells, the sky held a curious yellow tinge, closer at hand frost still lingered on the grass and the drystone walls but it was less sharp now though there was a raw coldness about the day.

If snow came it could make the journey to the hospital very difficult, perhaps impossible for her, since the farm was situated well away from the village and on a steep hill. Well, she would have to hope for the best, but she would set off earlier than she had intended and then at least Laurie would have a visit from her today. He would understand if she did not make it tomorrow because the farm had often been cut off by snow for a day or two in the past.

The dogs, having shared her breakfast, came to lick her hand. How glad Laurie would be to get back to them and to the rest of his animals.

'Your master will be home soon,' she told Chance and Risky. 'Laurie is coming home!' and they filled the bitingly cold air with their joyous barking as if they understood what she was saying.

From time to time as she gathered eggs and fed the hens, ironed pyjamas to take to the hospital for Laurie, washed the dishes and prepared a meal for the evening, she kept an eye on the weather. It was not improving, she knew, so she would be wise to start her journey to the hospital as soon as possible.

There was dampness in the air as she backed her car out of the garage on to the hill, a fine rain that would soon become snow. By the time she had driven through the village and headed for Middleby the sky was so dark that she switched on her headlights and increased her speed.

The snow had reached Middleby ahead of her, covering the hospital car park with a thin carpet of white which was already becoming slippery. It seemed to take her ages that day to walk down the long corridor to the small ward where Laurie was. Her hands felt clammy with nervousness and her heart was bumping unevenly when she reached the door of the ward.

Her anxiety increased when she saw that there were curtains drawn about Laurie's bed. She stopped in her tracks, wondering if she dared go beyond those curtains, or whether the nursing staff were coping with a fresh crisis in Laurie's condition. Then she saw with immense relief that Sister Campbell was emerging from behind them.

'Oh, hello!' There was a flustered air about the usually calm young Scotswoman. Her cheeks were quite pink and Amber was certain there was moisture lurking in the lovely dark-lashed eyes. Her alarm deepened.

'You're—you're a little earlier than usual today.'—Sister Campbell set her starched white cap straight on her crisp black curls and brushed away the tear that was poised to travel down her cheek.

'Yes, I came early because of the bad weather forecast. Is everything all right, Sister? With Laurie, I mean?'

The sister nodded, and smiled, which perplexed Amber even more, so that she went on hurriedly 'I've been worrying about how he would be when I got here. Has Zoe been in to see him yet?'

'Yes, she's been, and gone. You'd better go in and he'll tell you about it.'

'She told me last night that she was coming in today to tell him the truth. That's why I've been so worried about him,' Amber confessed.

Linda Campbell gave her a smile of quite dazzling radiance and said 'You can stop worrying now. It's all right. Laurie will tell you. I'll see you later, Amber.'

With that, she urged Amber through the nearest flowered curtain with a surprisingly firm hand, then hurried away.

Amber held her breath as she advanced towards the chair where Laurie sat. Amazingly, he was smiling a welcome for her. She allowed her breath to escape on a long sigh of relief.

'Hello,' he said in a cheerful voice. 'Did you enjoy the dance last night?'

'Yes.' She smiled back. 'Yes, I did.'

'Zoe told me she met you there,' her twin said now.

Amber swallowed. 'So she's been in to see you?'

He nodded. 'Yes, for the last time.'

Her throat went dry as she waited for him to go on and explain that remark. To break down, perhaps, and share his distress with her now that he knew his marriage was over.

'Oh, Laurie, I'm so sorry,' she burst out when she could bear the silence no longer.

'Don't be,' he said very quietly. 'I'm not.'

Her eyes widened. 'But I thought—I mean, we were dreading your remembering—Finding out that she had left you.'

Laurie put a hand on her own trembling fingers. 'Poor Amber! I've caused you so much worry these last few months. I'm really sorry about that. I was a fool to let myself go to pieces as I did over someone like her. I was a fool ever to fall for her in the first place, but I was just bewitched by her and I couldn't see what she was really like until it was too late. Lying here with nothing else to do but watch her, and listen to her, when she visited me made me realize that we had nothing left to share in the future.'

'Tom thought you had begun to remember what happened a day or two ago, before Zoe came to tell you she was leaving.' Her eyes searched his face for confirmation of this and she found herself marvelling at his calmness, his air of confidence.

'Yes, I did. There was something about the way I felt whenever Zoe was visiting me that made me very uneasy. I know I ought to have been glad to see her, the way I was always pleased when you or Tom came, but I never felt that way. In fact I began to dread her visits because there was a kind of resentment against her in my mind that made me feel guilty. I was dreading coming home and having to live with her at the farm.' He stopped and gave Amber a

146

rueful glance. 'Of course I didn't know that Zoe wasn't living at the farm with you and Tom. You were very careful to keep that from me, weren't you?'

Amber was confused. 'We only did what we thought was for the best, Laurie, when you were so ill. I was afraid of what would happen when you discovered the truth.'

'One thing I've had while I've been in hospital has been time to think, to sort out my own feelings and make adjustments to them. To make decisions too about what will happen when I get out of here.'

Amber sat down, knowing that at last she could shed at least some of her worries about Laurie and his future.

'We'll manage,' she assured him.

'Lambing will be starting soon and we'll need help then,' Laurie said. 'I was talking about it to Linda and she mentioned one of her ex-patients to me. He's a retired shepherd who is very lonely since his invalid wife died. Linda brought him in to see me and he's agreed to come and help us. He'll be glad of the company, he says, and he's willing to live in the holiday cottage rent free in exchange for looking after our sheep. You'll like him.'

Amber was puzzled. 'Linda? Do I know her?'

'Yes, of course! Linda Campbell, my favourite nurse.'

She smiled. 'Oh, I see.'

Now his eyes, resting on her face, asked for her understanding. 'Linda has become rather special to me since I began to get well, Amber. I know she's the sort of woman I ought to have married. It's too soon to make plans about that yet, except that I'd like you to ask Mr Beckwith to come in and see me about starting divorce proceedings. Will you ask him, please?'

'Yes, of course.' Amber was recalling Linda Campbell's radiant smile and the tear that had trembled on her cheek. 'I agree with you that she is a special person, but does she feel the same about you, Laurie?' she felt forced to ask.

'She says she does, but we've agreed to take our time about telling anyone except you, and to give ourselves the chance to get to know one another away from the hospital. I've asked her if she'll come and stay at the farm when I come home. She has a couple of weeks' holiday due to her in spring. She says she'll come then.'

Amber laughed. 'At least she knows what she's in for, being a farmer's daughter, if she takes you on! When did you manage to get all this sorted out?'

He grinned. 'This afternoon, just before you arrived and just after Zoe left.'

She laughed again. 'No wonder the curtains were drawn around your bed! And I thought you'd had a relapse—'

His face sobered. 'I can't wait to get home, now that my life is beginning to make sense again. I was so afraid, before,' he confessed.

'You'll soon be home. In a couple of weeks time, Mr Richards said.'

'I won't be able to do much at first, and I'll have to come back for physiotherapy, but I suppose there will be some bookkeeping to catch up on?'

'Not as much as you'd think. Rory helped me with that.' She saw him frown as she said that.

'I hope that doesn't mean you are getting involved with him again? I don't want you to get hurt again.'

'There's no chance of that. Not as far as Rory is concerned,' she assured him.

'I hope I didn't spoil anything for you up there in Scotland when you had to come racing down here to take over the farm, Amber?'

'No. There was no one special for me up there.'

There was someone special for her much closer at hand. An immense surge of joy filled her as she thought of Fergus. Wonderful, warm, caring, loving, Fergus, who made her laugh, and brought her comfort when she needed it most. Why had she sent him away last night in despair when she needed him so much? A longing came over her to be with Fergus that was so strong it would not be denied. Impatience brought her to her feet.

'I'm sorry I can't stay long today Laurie,' she said breathlessly. 'I have to get in touch with the vet as soon as possible.'

149

Her brother frowned. 'Why? Is there something wrong with the animals?'

Amber laughed joyously. 'No, but there's something wrong with me! Fergus, the vet, has been helping me at the farm, and I've fallen in love with him.'

Now Laurie grinned. 'So Tom was right!'

Amber stopped on her way out. 'What do you mean?'

'Tom said the vet had fallen for you, but you couldn't seem to make your mind up about him.'

'I have now! You'll need to work very hard on your physiotherapy, Laurie, so you can walk down the aisle with me to give me away at my wedding.'

'Don't make him wait too long,' Laurie warned her. 'Not on my account. You have to put your vet first now, not me.'

'I know,' she called over her shoulder as she dashed away from him, down the corridor and out of the hospital to the snow-covered car park.

Fergus had told her last night that he was taking the afternoon surgery at Middleby today. If she hurried she would just catch him there before he left. She must catch him, because she could not wait to tell him how much she loved him. How much she needed him. How much she longed to marry him.

Yet she could not hurry on roads that were by now treacherous with a few inches of frozen

150

snow. All she could do was move at crawling pace and hope he was still at the surgery. Of course she could telephone him from the farm when she got home but it would not be the same. She wanted to see him, touch him, be held by him.

When she at last reached the veterinary surgery on the edge of the market town she saw with acute disappointment that the car park was empty, and that no lights shone out from the building. She was too late. Fergus had gone, so she would have to head for home because Tom would be getting anxious about her as the weather worsened. She turned her car about with difficulty and joined the road to Edenby.

By now driving was a nightmare as the blizzard intensified and the wind grew stronger, hurling frozen snowflakes at her windscreen with such force that she gritted her teeth and forced herself to go on, slowly, so slowly that at least she had a chance of remaining on the icy road instead of ending up in a ditch. It was less than a dozen miles from Edenby to Middleby but she seemed to have been driving for hours. Her fingers felt numb and her head was aching with the effort of keeping her car on the road. She sent up a prayer of thanksgiving when she at last reached the village, then one for help as she faced the long, difficult climb that was three quarters of a mile along to Edengate Farm.

Once there she could not face turning the car in the banked up snow that was all about her. Instead she steered it into the parking place opposite the farm, behind a parked vehicle which already resembled an igloo. Some stranded motorist who dare not drive any further in such conditions, she guessed, and had taken shelter in her home. It had happened before in other winters. An extra guest to share the casserole she had left in the oven, she decided as she ploughed through a snowdrift to the back door.

Then the back door was opening and strong hands were drawing her into the kitchen. Warm hands that brushed the snow from her cheeks and held her firmly while her lips kissed again and again.

When she got her breath back she said 'Oh, Fergus, what are you doing here?'

'Waiting for you, my love. I left the surgery early because most of my clients seemed to have been frightened away by the weather. I came straight here because I wanted to be here when you came back from the hospital. I thought you might be upset if Laurie had taken his wife's departure badly and I wanted to be here to comfort you.'

'Oh Fergus,' she said again, this time with tears in her voice. 'I love you so much.'

'Do you?' He kissed her again, to make certain.

'Yes. I went to your surgery in Middleby to

tell you that, but of course you had gone.'

'I couldn't get here quickly enough to tell you that I didn't mean what I said last night. That I understand how you feel and I'll wait for you until Laurie can manage without you.'

Amber laughed. 'I don't think he'll need me for long. He was not upset about Zoe after all, because he's been realizing recently that he should never have married her, and he's been falling in love with his nursing sister at the hospital.'

Fergus grinned. 'So all's well with his world?'

'It will be, in time. Linda's a lovely girl, and she's a farmer's daughter too!'

'All's certainly well with my world,' Fergus said as he pulled her closer into his arms again. 'Now I've got you to share it with me.'